"Don't f[...]
Nick said intently

"You know as well as I do that we're still very much attracted to each other. It's always been there when we're together. Your hostility is just a defense against the truth."

"Are you trying to persuade me that maybe we should start where we left off two years ago?" Megan asked derisively. "Have a convenient affair, no strings attached and a friendly goodbye when the project is finished?"

"No, Megan," Nick said softly. "You may not believe this, but I never meant to hurt you."

"Well," Megan shrugged carelessly, "it hardly matters now. I was young and stupid, and it was a long time ago."

Nick's eyes met hers. "But not long enough."

KAREN VAN DER ZEE is an author on the move. Her husband's work as an agricultural adviser to developing countries has taken them to many exotic locations. The couple said their marriage vows in Kenya, and celebrated the birth of their first daughter in Ghana and their second in the United States, where they make their permanent home. The whole family spent two fascinating years in Indonesia. Karen has had several short stories published in her native Holland, and her modern romance novels with their strong characters and colorful backgrounds are enjoyed around the world.

Books by Karen van der Zee

Don't miss any of our special offers. Write to us at the following address for information on our newest releases.

Harlequin Reader Service
901 Fuhrmann Blvd., P.O. Box 1397, Buffalo, NY 14240
Canadian address: P.O. Box 603,
Fort Erie, Ont. L2A 5X3

KAREN VAN DER ZEE

shadows on bali

Harlequin Books

TORONTO • NEW YORK • LONDON
AMSTERDAM • PARIS • SYDNEY • HAMBURG
STOCKHOLM • ATHENS • TOKYO • MILAN

Harlequin Presents first edition November 1988
ISBN 0-373-11126-6

Original hardcover edition published in 1988
by Mills & Boon Limited

CHAPTER ONE

THE paper felt like gold in her hands.

It's too good to be true, Megan thought, riffling through the papers and finally stacking them neatly on the coffee-table. And you know what they say: If it looks too good to be true, it probably is!

A wonderful project, a great job, the perfect place. Bali. Who wouldn't want to spend a couple of years in a tropical paradise? And the job . . . the job seemed as if it had been designed just for her.

Something has to be wrong with it, she thought, frowning, staring at the paper. BALI, LOW COST HOUSING PROJECT, it said on the cover. PROJECT DESCRIPTION. She'd read it twice, the first time quickly, the second time more carefully. There was something about this paper, something familiar, yet she couldn't pinpoint it.

The high of excitement made her feel warm and restless all over. Community development adviser—it sounded wonderful. She'd be the person to figure out the local scene—how people lived, the type of houses they liked—then help the engineers use that information in their designs. The perfect job in the perfect place. Bali. She would love to go to Bali.

I deserve it, she told herself. I've done enough impossible jobs in impossible places in the last few years. I'm due a good one. International consulting was a fascinating field for building a career, the many frustrations well worth the excitement and interesting experiences.

She looked at her watch. Ten past eight! Good lord! She jumped up, rushed into the bedroom, stripped off her office clothes and got into the shower. For a fleeting moment she considered forgetting about the party and staying home, then discarded the idea. She'd worked like a maniac all week; a party would do her good.

Forty minutes later she was ready, dressed in her most sophisticated finery and made up beautifully, her face framed by a short, glossy cap of sleek brown har, her hazel eyes glittering with the excitement she felt at the job prospect.

'Boy, do I work fast, or what?' she asked her reflection in the mirror, and grinned. 'Knock 'em dead, kid!'

Corina, the hostess, greeted her with breathless enthusiasm, hugging her and pecking her on the cheek. The house was large and people were everywhere—in the living-room, family-room, dining-room and kitchen.

'Get yourself a drink,' Corina ordered. 'In the dining-room. And help yourself to the food, please.'

'Thanks.' Food—great. She'd forgotten to eat dinner as she read the project paper, and her stomach was beginning to protest.

She moved into the living-room, scanning the crowd for familiar faces. God, the clothes people wore to parties! Everything from faded jeans to gold lamé. Her gaze moved on and her heart made a sudden, sickening lurch.

Across the room, a man was looking at her: deep blue eyes, a face that was not handsome, but thoroughly masculine—a little rough around the edges, like a carving not quite finished. A mop of thick black hair. His penetrating gaze held hers, and she stood frozen to the floor, her legs unable to move.

She'd found a familiar face.

A face more familiar than any other, the only one she hadn't wanted to see.

Nick. Nick Donovan. He hadn't changed. He looked as she remembered him—tall and broad across the chest and shoulders, the black hair a little wild and unruly, the blue eyes as bright as ever in the dark face, the same square chin jutting out aggressively.

It had finally happened, this accidental meeting somewhere in Washington. Megan had had nightmares about this moment—wanting it, yet dreading it at the same time. She felt panic rise in her, felt her legs begin to tremble violently. She turned, rushed back into the hallway and collided head on with a silk-shirted chest.

'Sorry,'' she muttered, and fled. Finding the bathroom, she locked the door and leaned against it, trembling.

Nick was here at this party. She hadn't seen him for two years—two of the bleakest years of her life. She hadn't known he was back in town. The last she'd heard, he was in Thailand.

She went over to the sink, and ran cold water over her hands and wrists.

The time had finally arrived. It was inevitable. They moved in the same circles. They were bound to meet again some time, somewhere. Now she'd have to handle it. Prove to herself that she could. Prove to herself, and him, that he no longer meant anything to her.

I'm leaving, she thought, searching frantically for some excuse she could give Corina. She could not face Nick. She was shaking like a leaf.

You're a coward. You can't live like this. You'll never go to another party as long as he's in town. He might be back for good, then what will you do? Go into eternal hibernation?

Right now, hibernation seemed like a wonderful idea. Megan ran more cold water over her wrists.

Go and meet the ghost of the past. Smile at him and be polite. Do what you've wanted to do: be cool and indifferent and show him you didn't die of a broken heart and you're alive and well.

She took a deep breath, squared her shoulders and stepped out of the bathroom.

At the end of the hall was Nick, with a woman at his side. Her heart began to thud painfully. Her stomach felt as if she'd swallowed a lump of cement. She wondered if he were there by accident, or if he had known she was hiding in the bathroom. It hadn't been the first time she'd hidden from him in the bathroom.

Be cool! she admonished herself, glancing at the brunette next to him. An elegant blue dress hugged a tall, slender body. She was neither beautiful nor glamorous, yet she had an interesting face, with calm grey eyes. Was she his woman of the moment? She felt her stomach cramp at the thought.

'Hello, Megan.' He extended his hand and took hers.

'Hello, Nick.'

'How are you?'

'I'm fine, thank you,' she managed politely. His hand was warm and solid, his grasp firm. She felt herself grow hot and cold at the same time.

He held on to her hand and studied her with those bright blue eyes, and it was there again—that old familiar smile she could see in her sleep. That boyish, devilish, irresistible smile that started with the faint twitch of the left corner of his mouth, then crept into his eyes, where it lingered, tempting, seducing. The smile that made her anger melt, her irritation fade, her worry evaporate. The smile that made her warm and giddy. The smile that had made her fall in love with him.

It seemed an eternity before he let go of her hand. 'Let me introduce you,' he said, turning to the woman by his side. 'Maxie, this is Megan Opperman. Megan, Maxie Goodwin.'

They shook hands and smiled politely at each other.

'Megan and I used to work for the same company,' Nick

said smoothly.

Lord, he was cool! 'A long time ago,' Megan added.

Maxie nodded. Intelligent eyes looked at her searchingly. Then she turned to Nick. 'I need to find Richard—I'll see you later.' She disappeared into the dining-room.

Nick leaned casually against the wall. He was dressed in grey tailored trousers and a teal cashmere sweater. He never wore suits or ties if he could help it. Apparently, that hadn't changed. No doubt he was still the same man in other respects as well. It was a bitter thought.

Megan certainly wasn't the same, inwardly or outwardly. Her hair was short now, a sophisticated, stylish cut. Her heart was no longer soft and sentimental. It had undergone changes of its own. She was a different person—stronger, less vulnerable, or so she liked to tell herself. Her strong reaction to seeing Nick again made her wonder.

'You look beautiful,' he said.

The changes in her appearance apparently met with his approval, not that it mattered. 'Thank you.'

'It's been a long time. I've wondered how you were.'

He'd wondered how she was? His concern was touching! She felt an urge to hit him. 'I've been very well, thank you,' she answered evenly, determined not to show him anything of what went on in her mind.

'I heard you were in Africa for a year,' he continued. 'Chad, wasn't it?'

'Yes.'

'How did you like it?'

'Too much sand. How was Thailand?'

'Fascinating place. I'd go back tomorrow.'

Megan did not want to get involved in a lengthy discussion on the pros and cons of their respective jobs in alien climes. What she wanted was to get away as soon as possible, without appearing overly anxious.

'How's your father?'

She saw the narrowing of his eyes. His mouth hardened. 'He's fine,' he said curtly, the smile gone.

No improvement on the home front, she could tell. She felt a moment of regret for the old man who could not forgive his son for not wanting to take on the business he had built from the ground up.

She glanced around a little desperately. She wanted to get away. She's done the polite thing—asked how he was, how he liked Thailand and how his father was. That just about covered everything. She straightened, and smiled vaguely. 'I'm going to get a drink and something to eat before I faint.'

Someone tried to pass them in the narrow hallway, and she took advantage of it and escaped. Her legs were definitely not steady. She went in search of her coat and slipped out of the door without seeing Corina.

By the time she got back to her apartment she felt dizzy from hunger, or was it something else? She dropped her coat on a chair, took a frozen dinner out of the freezer and shoved it into the microwave, just as the phone rang.

Megan picked up the receiver, kicked off her shoes and dropped down on the couch.

'Hello?'

'Megan? It's me, Christa. Listen, when is Jason coming back?'

'Next week.' He'd been gone several days now, attending some conference in New York. Megan watched raindrops slither down the window. It had just started raining. A bad November this year—lots of rain and wind, and flooding in low-lying areas.

'Good. What are you doing for Thanksgiving?'

'Work. Wash underwear.'

'You can't do that.'

'Just watch me!' laughed Megan.

'Come home with me,' Christa invited. 'It's only a two-hour drive. My mother loves welcoming strays into the bosom of her family for Thanksgiving. A family tradition.'

'Gee, thanks. I'd never thought of myself as a stray.' Megan's mother had recently moved to California to be with her son and his family. Going home for Thanksgiving, from Washington, was a costly and time-consuming undertaking.

'I'll pick you up at seven on Wednesday,' Christa went on.

'I didn't say I'd come.'

'My mother's turkey is famous. Her stuffing is out of this world. Her pumpkin pie is the best in the state.'

'I'll be ready.'

Christa laughed. 'Also, my handsome brother, the almost-doctor, is coming.'

Megan rolled her eyes. 'I'll do my best to win him over. How about a discreet little seduction scene right in front of the family.'

'Oh, Megan! There's got to be somebody better than Jason for you! I don't know why you do this to yourself! First that jerk from the State Department. What was his name? Donald? And now this insipid . . .'

'Jason suits me fine,' said Megan firmly.

'He's as interesting as an unsalted egg!'

'I'm sorry you feel that way. I'm rather fond of him myself. He's very comfortable to have around.'

'Like a mink coat.'

Megan switched the receiver to her other ear and tugged her leg under her. 'More like a rabbit, actually,' she said.

Christa groaned. 'Jason is an idiot.'

'But a nice one. He takes care of my dry-cleaning and feeds me chicken soup when I'm sick.'

'He sounds like a wife!'

Megan smiled into the receiver. 'Don't tell me you're jealous. It's the dream of every career woman I know—to have a wife. It's great. You should try it.'

'Megan! Why can't you ever be serious?' pleaded Christa.

'I'm deadly serious.'

'There's no talking to you!'

'You've certainly given it the old college try—insulting my man. If I were a lesser woman I'd never speak to you again.'

'Megan! I just don't *understand* you when it comes to men! What's wrong with *love* and . . . and *passion?*' Christa liked passion. It was right there in her voice. Megan smiled to herself. She could almost see Christa at the other end of the line—bushy red hair standing on end, her free hand gesturing wildly. Everything Christa did was infused with enthusiasm and spirit—her work, her love-life.

'Nothing's wrong with it, Christa,' she said, 'It's just not for me.'

'What do you *mean* by that? Why are you searching out men like this David and Jason? It doesn't make sense! Remember that tall guy with the accent we met at that party some months ago? What was he, French?'

'French Canadian. Philippe Durand, from the Embassy.'

'Right. Now, I know he was after you. You went out with him a couple of times and then you dropped him.'

Megan sighed. 'He was very nice, but . . .'

'*Nice?* That's the understatement of the year! The man was interesting, smart, sophisticated, sexy as hell . . .'

'You're right,' Megan agreed.

'So you dropped him.'

'He was much too intense for me.'

There was a short pause. Christa's frustration vibrated across the line. '*Megan, he was a man!*'

Megan closed her eyes wearily. 'Will you do me a favour, Christa?'

'Mind my own business?'

'Smart girl.'

Christa sighed, defeated. 'All right, all right. Anyway, what's new? Haven't talked to you for ages.'

'I'm thinking about a new job, but don't tell a soul.'

'Why not? Some head hunter after you?' asked Christa.

'Yes. CCD—Creative Community Development. A low-cost housing project on Bali,' Megan told her.

'Bali! Why don't they ever send me to places like Bali?'

Megan grinned into the phone. 'Because you'd never come back. And besides, I'm not there yet. They still have to win the contract.'

'They'll get it.'

'What makes you say that?'

'I know about that project,' said Christa.

It didn't surprise her. Working for the Asia Bureau at the Agency for International Development, there was little Christa didn't know about what went on in the Far East.

'They've got an inside track. I know the guy who designed it, Nick Donovan. Ever met him?'

Megan's heart turned over in her chest. For a moment, it wsa impossible to breathe. Too good to be true, she'd thought, and sure enough it was.

It took an effort to compose herself. 'Yes, I've met him.' Her voice sounded strange in her own ears. She cleared her throat. 'Well, we'll see. I've got to go now—my Lean Cuisine is perishing in the oven. Thank for the invitation.'

It was clear to Megan now why she'd thought there was something familiar about the paper. It was the writing. *Nick's* writing. He had a style of his own. Why hadn't she known right away? She picked up the paper and looked at it frowning. There was a page missing. The page with the credits which should state Nick's name. She hadn't even noticed.

She shrugged and straightened her shoulders. To hell with Nick! She didn't care; she wanted the job. Nobody, not even Nick Donovan, was going to stand in her way.

Brave thoughts, so why were her hands shaking? Why was her heart fluttering in her chest like some nervous bird? She stared at the paper on the table as if it were a poisonous snake.

Before tonight, she hadn't seen Nick in over two years. She'd heard of him, of course. The international consulting business was a small world. She knew he'd spent a year in Pakistan and had travelled extensively in various places in the Far East, including Thailand, doing short-term work.

I probably won't have anything to do with him, she decided. It isn't a big project, and someone of Nick's experience probably won't deal with it personally. He'll be out doing something larger and more important. It's safe enough.

The next Monday she called CCD's office to make an appointment for an interview.

'How is two o'clock tomorrow?' the assistant asked, the young voice cool and businesslike.

They certainly weren't wasting time! 'Fine, I'll be there. Who will I talk to?'

'Nick Donovan.'

Megan closed her eyes and bit her lower lip, hard. 'Thank you.' She replaced the receiver and sat still for a moment, trying to calm her nerves.

Did Nick know he was meeting her tomorrow? It seemed unlikely that he would not be aware of the people who had been contacted in connection with his project. He *had* to know.

Oh, damn! she thought. Maybe I should just call the whole thing off.

But she didn't. There was only one way to deal with this—like a professional, stone-cold sober. After all, Nick Donovan was part of her past. He had no place in her life now, and she had reconciled herself with that truth. Yet she woke up in the middle of the night, shaking and filled with a nameless dread.

At three minutes to two that afternoon, she walked into CCD's office, dressed fit to kill—the career woman, straight off the pages of a high fashion magazine.

'Mr Donovan is expecting you,' the receptionist said, looking her over enviously. 'His office is down the hall, third door on the left. Here, let me take your coat.'

Heels clicking on the wooden floor, Megan made her way down the hall. The door was open, and loud voices reached her ears as she approached Nick's office. One of them was Nick's, and it wasn't friendly.'

'I will not, and I repeat, *I will not* have my name on that report! I will not have my name connected with that miserable piece of work! The whole thing is going to collapse around him and we're going to look like a bunch of amateurs!'

She stood in the door, heart hammering frantically. *Now stop it!* she admonished herself. Get a grip on yourself! He stood in the middle of the room, hands on his hips, black hair falling over his forehead, blue eyes icy with anger, as he glared at the man standing only feet away from him.

He wore a wool sweater with a blue shirt underneath, and dark trousers. No tie. Even after two years he still looked painfully familiar.

Nick became aware of her presence, and for a moment their eyes met. Megan's heart began to pound wildly. His expression, as he looked at her, didn't change, but for a moment there was a pause in the flow of words, and a sudden nerve-tingling stillness hung in the room.

Then he looked back at the other man. 'My decision is final. I don't give a damn what they do about it, but if the arrogant son of a bitch is determined to undermine the evaluation, I won't have a thing to do with it. And now, if you'll excuse me, I have an appointment.' He turned to Megan. 'Come in, please.'

He gestured her in, holding the door open for the man to pass, then closed it firmly. He turned to face her.

'Hello, Megan,' he said evenly. 'We meet again.'

'Yes.'

His eyes ran over her in quick appraisal. She wondered what he was thinking. He'd never seen her in a suit—trim, businesslike, with a simple white blouse and high-heeled pumps; she'd gone for lace and flounces back in the days they'd known each other. Romantic, feminine clothes, soft colours. *Sentimental slob,* Megan derided herself.

'Please, sit down.' He waved at a chair, seating himself in the one behind his desk. He raked his fingers through his hair, pushing it back from his forehead, an oddly familiar gesture. How many times had she seen him do that?

For a moment he studied a paper in front of him, frowning. *Maybe he's uneasy, too.* The thought made her laugh inwardly. Nick was never uneasy. Nick always knew what he wanted and always got it.

He raised his head and looked at her without particular expression. Good, she thought. He's in his businessman mode. I can handle that. She'd wondered how he would conduct this meeting—in his casual, jocular manner, or in a more professional way. With Nick, you could never tell. There were several different facets to his personality, seemingly contradictory, but somehow well integrated. He could be tough and businesslike and stand for no nonsense, as she had just witnessed. People who knew him in a work situation often had no idea that there was another very different part to his character. He could be playful and fun and refuse to take anything seriously.

'Your résumé is very impressive,' he commented. 'Three months in Sierra Leone. A year in Chad—interesting project, that one. Several short-term stints in the Caribbean. I didn't know they were doing much rebuilding of housing there.' He put the paper down. 'You've been busy these last couple of years.'

She certainly had. And a good thing too. 'Thank you,' she said calmly, determined to be cool and professional. There wsa no reason not to be. Nick Donovan was history.

Megan glanced around the office. There were books and papers everywhere—in bookcases, on tables, in piles on the floor. A map of the world hung on one wall, a map of Africa on another. A computer, switched on, adorned a table which was pushed crookedly into a corner. An office used by itinerant consultants, obviously. Everybody used it and nobody claimed it.

'I'm glad to see you've done so well.'

Oh, he was, was he? What had he expected? Work was all she'd had after he'd left. For six months she had driven herself past every limit, forcing herself to forget him. Then one hot and steamy night she had collapsed, alone, in a damp little hotel room in Sierra Leone. She had cried and raged for endless days and nights. She hadn't eaten or slept, had lost ten pounds, until finally, exorcised, she'd managed to get control of herself again. She'd taken a long-term assignment in Chad and gone on with her life, a life that still seemed as barren as the desert that made up most of the country.

'Have you ever been to Bali?' he asked.

'Only passing through. I stayed with a friend for a week in Denpasar.' She'd rented a motor-cycle and toured the island, falling in love with it. A luscious green paradise of rice paddies, Hindu temples, shrines and *gamelan* music.

'What did you think of the project description? Any comments?'

'I like the concept, but it doesn't say much about the building designs or form of construction. It's an important issue that needs consideration before implementation gets under way.

He nodded. 'It's part of the implementation. It will be

your job to help us figure it out. I don't foresee major problems with it.'

You might be surprised, Megan thought wryly, but refrained from saying so.

Nick examined her résumé. 'Tell me something about that Ford Foundation project in Chad. It says here you were the administrative assistant. How did you get involved with the housing project?'

'By coincidence, actually. One of the consultants got sick, and they had to medi-vac him out. I helped out as much as I could, and got more and more involved. I enjoyed it, and the other people were wonderful.' Megan went on to explain, aware all the while of his blue gaze intent on her face.

'What issues do you think are important in designing this type of housing?'

'I think it's important to take into consideration the traditional housing people are used to, the cultural aspects of design, the way they live, the use of local material, that sort of thing.'

He frowned. 'What about the budget, time and efficiency?'

'Well, of course. But we have to think of the other aspects, too. To just slap down some sort of a four-wall unit and call it a house is a terrible mistake, and one that has been made too often.'

The questions went on. It was like any other interview she'd done before, only with undercurrents of uneasiness flowing between them. Once, they'd known each other very well; now, they were both pretending this was nothing more than a business meeting between strangers.

'It's a two, probably three-year contract,' Nick said. 'Do you have any commitments that might require you to leave the job before its completion?'

'No.'

One dark eyebrow rose in question. 'What about this Jason Michaels?'

How did he know about Jason? It took a moment for Megan to gather her thoughts. 'Jason Michaels is none of your business.' Her voice was under perfect control. The message was not lost on him, yet he didn't miss a beat.

'With any luck, we'll know for sure if we win the contract in two or three months. Would you be able to leave within a month after that?'

'Yes. But I'd appreciate it if my participation in this bid could be kept confidential, at least for the time being.'

'Of course.'

'There's something else I'd like to know. Did you know they'd contacted me for the job when we met at the party last Friday night?'

'Yes.'

'Why didn't you mention it?'

'I didn't want you to know I was involved in it before you'd made up your mind about the project itself.'

'So that's why the page with the credits was missing!'

Nick made no reply to that, but from the look in his eyes she knew she was right. She wasn't sure what to think about it, but decided to drop the subject.

'May I ask if you have anyone to head up the project?'

He gave her a sharp look, then glanced back down at the papers in front of him. 'I've spoken to Tom Marsden about the project. Do you know him?'

'Tom Marsden?' She felt a jolt of happy surprise. 'Yes, I do! I worked for him in Sierra Leone. He's great!' For a moment, her professional cool got lost in her enthusiasm. 'I'd love to work for him again!'

'Good. We've lined up a financial analyst and we're still looking for a construction engineer, but they won't come in until we're ready to write up the final project presentation. We have some good possibilities. We need to do some interviewing before we know for sure. '

'Anyone else for my position?'

He gave a crooked smile. 'No. You're it. And, if you want the job, it's yours.'

She felt a rush of excitement. 'Thank you.' Then she frowned. 'How did I get to be called about this job?' she asked. 'I don't know any of CCD's people very well.'

He shrugged. 'You know how it goes. We call around, follow leads, ask for recommendations, go through our files. Somewhere out there, you connected with the system. And you seemed to be the best candidate. It's difficult coming up with people with appropriate experience.' He closed her file and put it on a pile. 'I'll let you know when I have more information on the timing and so forth.'

'Thank you.' She picked up her bag and came to her feet. Nick pushed his chair back, came around the desk and faced her, holding out his hand.

'It was good seeing you again, Megan.' His grip was cool and firm, and his eyes looked directly into hers, as if waiting for some sort of personal response.

She had none to offer. She forced herself to smile politely. 'I'll hear from you, then.' She extracted her hand. 'Goodbye, Nick.'

Not until she was back outside in the crisp autumn air did she realise how very tense she had been. She took in several deep gulps of cool air as she walked to the car park to get her car. She'd done an admirable job, had been all cool, calm professionalism, but underneath the tension had flourished. And the old, familiar pain was back.

Damn! she thought, reaching for her car key. He can still do it to me!

'Is it true you and Nick Donovan had a thing for each other some years back?' Christa asked, peering through the windscreen into the dark, rainy night.

'Where did you get that idea?' Megan pulled her coat closer around her. The heater in the car wasn't working and she couldn't wait to get to Christa's house and warm her icy feet.

'From Nick himself.'

'He *told* you?' gasped Megan.

'Well, not in so many words. I surmised it. You know how I am at surmising.'

'And at imagining and presuming and embroidering and making up facts!'

'I'm very creative that way.'

'When did you see Nick?'

'At a party on Saturday night.'

He was making the rounds, it seemed. Two parties in a row. Funny, he hadn't been that much of a party-goer before.

'I run into him now and then.' Christa continued. 'Some man, all right. Why did you ever let him go?'

'I didn't let him go. He let me go.'

Christa whistled through her teeth. 'Ouch!' She gave Megan a quick, sideways glance. 'Why have you never mentioned him to me?'

'It never came up. Besides, he's not worth mentioning.' Christa and she had been friends only a year, although sometimes it seemed they'd known each other for ever.

'Oh, but I disagree there.'

Megan smiled. 'Of course you do, Christa.'

'What's wrong with him?' asked her friend.

'He's a selfish, insensitive, arrogant bastard.'

'Funny, I wouldn't say that at all.'

'What would you say?'

'He's charming, fun, intelligent, interesting.'

'That's got nothing to do with it.' The truth was, Christa was right. Nick was all that, too. He was the most interesting, irrestistible, infuriating man she had ever known.

He had never divulged much of his inner thoughts and feelings, and it had often bothered her. He would get deeply involved in his work, to the exclusion of everything else. He would be irritable, wouldn't notice her and become cool and aloof. She'd feel neglected and hurt. At other times, he'd be outgoing and entertaining, charming her with that funny, irrestistible smile that melted all her anger and hurt. She'd feel loved again.'

'How long did you know each other?' asked Christa.

'A year and a half.'

There was a pause. 'What did you think of him when you saw him again?'

Megan shrugged. 'Nothing. He hasn't changed much. He's getting a little grey at the temples—worry, I hope.'

'Ah! I detect a touch of rancour! Do you still love him?'

'You've got to be kidding!'

'Well, of course, I am. You love the jerk.'

'Madly,' said Megan drily.

Christa gave a derisive snort. 'Yeah, I've noticed!'

Megan rolled her yes, but said nothing.

'We'll be there in half an hour,' Christa told her.

'Dead or alive.'

'Sam will revive you.'

'Sam? Oh, the almost-doctor.'

Sam himself opened the door for them and carried in their luggage when they finally got to the house. He was tall and blond, like a Viking, and his grip practically crushed Megan's hand when they were introduced. She hoped he was more gentle with the babies and children he would deal with as a paediatrician.

He put her in front of a raging fire, brought her a drink and sat down next to her on the couch, boldly looking her over.

'You're very pretty.'

'Thank you,' said Megan, inclining her head slightly.
'I'm glad my sister was right for once.'

'Oh?'

'She keeps bringing over her friends, and they never turn out to be as great and gorgeous as she claims them to be. The last one had huge limpid eyes and looked like a cocker spaniel.'

Megan laughed. 'Poor girl!'

'Poor me! I had to go out with her.'

'Maybe she had a great personality.'

'She giggled and wagged her tail a lot.'

'That doesn't sound like one of Christa's friends.'

Sam gave a boyish grin. 'I was making it up. But you, you are definitely worth looking at.' His gaze slid appreciatively over her. 'Gorgeous brown eyes, sensuous mouth, long legs, great b . . . Well, I won't go on.'

'Please don't.' She straightened away from him a little and looked at him sardonically. 'Christa has a plan for us, are you aware of that?'

His eyes laughed into hers. 'Quite.'

'She's on a rescue mission. She's not enthralled with my latest choice of man, and is determined to save me from myself.'

He nodded. 'I heard.'

'What did she tell you?'

'That your present beau is a wet noodle.'

Megan sipped her drink, making no reply.

'Is she right?'

She smiled. 'No. He's the quiet, unassuming type, and he wears glasses and has the misfortune of being a professor of English. He has a great sense of humour, once you get to know him, which Christa hasn't. In your dear sister's opinion, anybody who's not famous, rich, of royal blood, brilliant, flamboyantly artistic, or a combination of these, is relegated to idiot status.'

'Woody Allen is famous, rich *and* artistic, and he's an idiot of the highest calibre.'

'Tell that to Christa.' Megan finished her drink and put the glass on the table. Her toes were thawing out and she was beginning to feel warm.

Sam's eyes settled on her lips. 'So, what are we going to do?'

'About what?'

'About Christa's plans for us?'

'What do you think we ought to do?'

He grinned. 'I think, to hell with it, let's make her happy.' He leaned closer, reaching out for her, and she put up her hands and stopped what was obviously going to be a passionate embrace, just as Christa came into the room to watch the scene.

'No go, Doctor.'

He made a face at Christa and shrugged. 'I tried,' he said apologetically, 'but she won't co-operate.'

It was not until late January that Megan heard from Nick Donovan again.

She'd just returned from three weeks in the Caribbean, doing a preliminary study on the rebuilding of the housing destroyed by hurricanes the previous summer. The weather had been gorgeous, the sea warm.

In shrieking contrast, Washington in January was the pits. That morning she'd slithered to the office over icy roads, had had an argument with her boss, and her computer had broken down so she hadn't been able to finish her report.

Nick's voice over the telephone jolted her out of her angry preoccupation with her problems. Her heart jumped into her throat at the sound of his voice.

'I wonder if we could meet for a drink after work,' he said.

'Why?'

'To talk. There are some things we need to go over before you go out there.'

'Shouldn't we wait to see if you win the bid?'

'We'll win it.'

Nick had never suffered from a lack of self-confidence. He usually got what he wanted. And got rid of what he didn't want, she added to herself.

'All right. When?'

'Tonight.'

She sighed. 'Fine, but I won't have much time. I'm meeting someone for dinner at seven-thirty and I can't get out of here until six.'

'Jason Michaels, by any chance?'

'None of your business,' she snapped.

Nick laughed softly. 'Touchy, touchy!'

She ignored that. 'Where do you want to meet?'

'You know the Exchange? I'll meet you there at six-fifteen.'

'All right. See you later.'

The phone rang five minutes after she'd finished talking to Nick. It was Jason, telling her that something had come up and that he couldn't meet her for dinner that night.

Great, she thought, putting the phone down. One more TV dinner this week. If I still have the stomach for it after I've had my session with Nick, that is.

The Exchange was a piano bar with a relaxing atmosphere. The music stayed quietly in the background, so that talking and listening were not a major strain on the vocal cords, ears or nerves.

Nick was already there when Megan arrived. She spotted him in one of the far corners, leaning back in his chair, long legs stretched out. Her heart made the old familiar flutter of recognition. *Cool it!* she told herself. He straightened when he noticed her, and watched her as she walked toward him across the length of the room. She didn't like his eyes on her, but there was little she could do about it.

'Hello, Megan.' He held out a chair for her.

'Hi.' She sat down, putting her coat and bag on the chair next to her.

'You look different,' he commented. 'I keep thinking how different you look.'

She raised her eyebrows. 'I do? Must be old age creeping up on me.' She'd actually discovered her first grey hair a week or so ago. At twenty-seven, it had come as a shock. She'd searched for more, but found none. The rest of her hair was still its original dark, glossy brown.

'You had your hair cut.'

'It's more practical that way. I was afraid it would grow mould when I was in Sierra Leone a couple of years ago! The place is like a Turkish bath.' He had liked her long hair, thick and heavy. Maybe that, too, had been a reason to get rid of it. Like she'd got rid of her apartment. Too many memories.

The waitress came to take their drink orders.

'Chablis?' Nick asked. It was what she's always ordered in the time they'd known each other.

'I'll have a sherry—medium dry.'

Nick gave a crooked little grin. 'Sherry—very civilised.'

'Isn't it?'

'I'll have a bourbon on the rocks,' he told the waitress, who scribbled it down and hurried away.

'You haven't changed,' Megan commented. 'Still drinking bourbon.'

He didn't reply, but put his elbows on the table and leaned his chin on his folded hands.

'I thought you'd be married by now,' he remarked.

He had to be kidding! She leaned back in her chair. 'I knew *you* wouldn't be.'

He winced. She couldn't believe it when she saw it—as if she'd touched a nerve. He didn't answer, and Megan looked away. She hadn't come here to answer personal questions or reminisce about the good old days. This was a business meeting. Everything else was irrelevant. She could almost feel herself grow hard and cold inside, blocking out memories and emotions. She looked at him as if he truly were a stranger, and an odd expression crossed his face. Sadness, regret. Maybe she had imagined it, because a moment later his face looked quite unmoved.

'I wasn't very good marriage material, I'm sure you agree,' Nick said lightly. 'Very selfish, unstable. Always on the road, wanting to see what else there was to discover in the world and avoiding ties and commitments.' He shook his head in self-deprecation and took a swallow of his drink. 'A worthless character, don't you agree?'

'Quite.' She wondered what the reason was for his spiel. A form of apology? A way of excusing himself, after two years?

He studied her for a moment. 'Not like you, of course. You were very different—a nest builder. Lots of flowers and plants and cosy cushions and schmaltzy music. Your cooking left something to be desired, most of the time, I must admit that. But then nobody is perfect, right?' He smiled charmingly. 'I'm surprised to find you haven't married. I thought you'd be knee-deep in nappies by now, singing nursery songs. Instead, I find you wandering the world on your own. You turned career girl, and a promising career it seems to be.' He took another swallow. 'Interesting.'

'I didn't come here to discuss my character, or yours,' she said coldly. 'You wanted to talk to me about the job.'

Nick's face sobered and he didn't immediately answer. 'I hurt you very badly, didn't I?' he asked at last, his voice low.

She shrugged. 'I don't remember. It's a long time ago. And let's get back to business, shall we?'

'All right.' He crossed his arms and leaned them on the

table. 'You're still interested?'

'Of course. You know as well as I do that this job is perfect for me. I'd have to be crazy not to want it.'

He nodded slowly. 'We have the rest of the team lined up for the proposal.' He picked up a file that had been lying on the table. 'These are the résumés. I want your comments on them.'

Megan gave him a sharp look. He could have sent copies to her in the post weeks ago. She could have talked to him over the phone. What kind of nonsense was this? Or was he still checking her out? Making sure he hadn't made a mistake? I'm not going to worry about it, she thought, opening the file. If he wants to change his mind, let him go ahead. What do I care?

A whole lot, she answered herself. You want the job, don't you?

She glanced through the papers in the file, then looked up, to find him watching her. 'Did you get Tom Marsden for project director?'

Nick straightened in his chair, his eyes not leaving her face. 'No. He got an offer from the World Bank.'

'You found somebody else?'

'Yes.'

She frowned, impatient. 'Who?'

'Me.'

CHAPTER TWO

MEGAN'S heart sank, and her hands clenched under the table. She no longer felt cold and detached. It was the worst possible news. '*You?* For project director?' Her tone made the idea sound rather distasteful, which, in a way, it was. But it was more than that. It was a disaster. In the position of project director, Nick would be her boss.

'There seems to be no other way.' He was observing her closely, and she forced herself to relax her fingers. She leaned back in her chair, trying to look casual and under control, trying to hide the turmoil in her mind.

'Aren't you a bit overqualified and overpriced for the job?'

He shrugged. 'I designed the project myself, and it's a damned good one, if not very impressive politically. I don't want some incompetent to ruin it.'

And in the whole world another competent and qualified candidate was not to be found? How stupid did he think she was? She gave him a sceptical look and his mouth twitched.

'We were in a time squeeze. We had to get the proposal out and we had no other strong candidates.'

It sounded plausible enough, yet she knew he was lying and she wondered why.

The drinks were delivered, along with a dish of salty nibbles. She took some and chewed, trying to evaluate the situation.

'Why are you taking this assignment?' she asked at last. 'Apart from the reasons you mentioned, which I find a little weak, why do you want to go to Bali? I can't imagine it would do much for your career.'

Nick took a swallow from his drink. 'It's a very romantic place.'

'So it is.' But what that had to do with anything was a mystery to her. Romance had never been one of the priorities in his life, but she knew better than to point that out.

'It's a luscious green paradise,' he continued. 'Idyllic, peaceful.'

She nodded. 'That, too.' She raised her brows, waiting for more.

He gave her an amused little smile. 'That's not good enough?'

'Not by a long shot.'

'All right, then. The truth is that I need a change.'

He needed a change. From what? From the high-powered, high-pressure jobs he always seemed to end up with? But that was what he thrived on. Or at least that was the way it used to be. She didn't believe him for a moment, but his reasons mattered less than the fact that he seemed determined to go to Bali.

So, now what? She was tempted to tell him she was no longer interested, paradise or no, career or no career. There was no way she was going to live on a tropical island with him for the next two or three years and work with him every day. Yet her pride fought heroically with her common sense. What would he think if she withdrew now? That she was still too much affected by him to be able to work with him? She wouldn't give him the satisfaction. And, apart from all the emotional considerations, taking the position would be a positive career move. She needed the job.

'Do you foresee any problems with the two of us working together?' he asked, as if guessing her thoughts.

Her shrug was light and casual. 'I'm sure we can deal with any professional problems. There are bound to be some.'

'I don't mean professionally. On a small island like Bali we can't avoid having a personal relationship as well.'

'I'm sure I can handle it,' said Megan, with just a hint of mockery in her voice. She picked up her sherry and took a sip.

'I was afraid you'd change your mind about going.'

She cocked one eyebrow. 'You flatter yourself. You walked out on me two years ago, Nick. You didn't honestly expect me to be still pining for you, did you?'

You smother me, he had said. You love me too much. The memory still hurt. She'd been too affectionate, too clinging, too demanding for his comfort. Nick didn't want to be tied down. He felt trapped, he'd said. So he had left. Megan had been devastated by his rejection of her and her love. She had loved him as deeply and honestly as she had been capable of, and it hadn't been enough. That had been the worst part—knowing that the best she had to give had not been good enough for Nick Donavan.

Well, she wouldn't make that mistake again. She'd turned the lock on that part of her feelings. She was no longer the sentimental fool who thrived on giving and receiving loving hugs and kisses, romantic meals for two, champagne in bed, schmaltzy love poems. It had all been wasted on a man like Nick, who didn't care for a demonstrative, clinging female in his life.

Two years was a long time. She was over Nick Donovan. She had stopped pining for him long ago.

'No,' he said slowly, 'I didn't think you were still pining for me, Megan.'

'Oh, I did for a while, you know. I cried for a week, or almost a week, anyway. Then I went to a party on Saturday and met someone else.' She smiled. 'So it wasn't too bad.'

He nodded. 'I can imagine,' he said drily. 'Still, I wasn't sure you'd be willing to spend a couple of years in my presence. I assume you don't have many favourable feelings towards me. It might not affect our working relationship positively.'

'And we don't want the project to suffer, do we? Well, don't worry about it. I don't think there'll be a problem. And if *you* are not comfortable with the situation, you can find someone else for my job.' She managed to sound calm and unperturbed.

'I want you.'

Megan's heart contracted at the words, as if a big hand had squeezed out the life in her. She looked at Nick, but his face was inscrutable. Words, just words. He wanted her—for the job, that was. He hadn't wanted her in his life. With an effort, she pushed the bitter thought back.

'And I want the job.'

For an endless, silent moment, he looked into her eyes. 'Then we'd better make it work, hadn't we?' he said lightly.

'Right.' Sipping her sherry, Megan began to study the résumés of the other two candidates, both of them short-termers who wouldn't be on the scene until later. There was a John Patterson, a construction engineer, and Maxie Goodwin, a financial analyst. Maxie Goodwin. She remembered the name, the face, the calm grey eyes. She felt a twinge of suspicion. Was she in the contract because Nick wanted her with him, or because she was a genuine candidate for the job?

Without looking up, she read through the paper. Maxie was good, very good. She was one of CCD's regular employees and had done several similar jobs.

She handed Nick the file. 'They seem very good, both of them.'

'Yes, I agree.' They discussed the résumés, and Nick ordered more drinks. The bar was getting crowded; people came and went—businessmen, yuppies, a swarthy man in a fez, a bald woman with a silk bandeau around her head and long, showy ear-rings. Her drink finished, Megan pushed the glass aside.

'I'd better go now.'

He looked at his watch. 'You're late for your dinner.'

'It was cancelled, actually. Thank you for the drinks.' She was about to stand up when he reached over and took her hand to detain her. A tingle went down her spine.

'Have dinner with me.' His eyes held hers, and her heart lurched. The warmth of his hand, holding hers, flooded all through her. Her throat went dry. The blue eyes held laughter, seduction, a plea.

'There's a little place, not far from here . . .'

Megan extracted her hand and swallowed hard. 'No, thanks,' she said calmly. 'I'd better go home and do some work.' She came to her feet and picked up her coat and bag.

He was suddenly right in front of her. 'Megan, do we have to be so goddamned polite to each other?'

Somehow, she found a measure of composure and looked at him, coolly surprised. 'What would you prefer?' she asked.

'I'm giving you a friendly invitation to dinner. You might consider accepting it in that spirit.'

'And then what? We talk about the good old days? No, thanks.' This time the bitterness was obvious in her voice, and she hated herself for giving it away.

'After two years, we ought to be able to have dinner without throwing knives at each other, don't you think? We should be able to come up with topics of discussion other than our previous relationship.' Nick frowned in concentration. 'Let's see now . . . there's the weather, Bali, politics.'

How civilised! Well, she didn't have the stomach for it. She didn't want to be around him if she could help it. That was all there was to it.

'I'm sure we can, but tonight it's quite impossible.'

'All right, as you please.' His voice was cool. He fished

some notes out of his pocket and dropped them on the table, then picked up his trench coat and followed her out the door.

It was raining and very windy. He walked with her to her car, and waited for her to open it and climb in.

'I'll talk to you later. Goodnight, Megan.'

'Goodnight.' She started the engine and let it warm up for a minute. Then, slowly, she backed out of the space, seeing Nick in her rear-view mirror as he opened the door to his own car. It was a blue Volvo, the same one he'd had two years ago.

She'd forgotten to lower the thermostat when she'd left that morning, and it was toasty warm in her apartment. She took off her suit, took a shower and washed her hair. Draped in an aqua caftan, a towel around her hair, she went to the kitchen to examine the possibilities for dinner.

She was inspecting the contents of the freezer, which looked decidedly unpromising, when the doorbell rang.

In front of the door was Nick, carrying a white paper bag, a boyish, taunting grin on his face, challenging her.

'Delivery,' he said, holding it out to her. 'Dinner for two.' He pushed past her and closed the door. 'You're losing all your precious heat. May I take off my coat?'

'I didn't invite you in,' Megan said icily.

'I'm aware of that. However, the more I think about it, the more I feel we should figure out our relationship before we get on a plane to Bali.'

He shrugged out of his coat, draped it over a chair and sat down. He looked around, his eyes taking in the casual, comfortable furniture, lingering on the bright, bold West Indian paintings, the Chinese rug she'd bought in Hong Kong, the large antique coffee-table she would refinish one day.

'Nice place. Why did you move?'

Megan glared at him without answering. Why did he

think she'd moved? After he'd left, she couldn't bear to live on in the place they'd shared.

He seemed unperturbed. 'Sorry I barged in like that, but I had the feeling it was the only way I was going to get past that door. Now, smile and have something to eat before it gets cold, if it isn't already.' He opened the bag, spread napkins on the coffee-table and took out hamburgers and french fries.

She quirked in a mocking eyebrow. 'You're sure losing your touch. Take-out *hamburgers?*'

'You had something better planned?' From his expression, she knew he had grave doubts. She was no cook and her reliance on frozen dinners and a microwave oven was not unknown to him.

She shrugged. 'Not hamburgers, anyway.'

'I bet not. Not fast enough.' Nick surveyed the food on the table. 'And what's wrong with hamburgers?' he challenged. 'It's a staple of the American diet. Where would we be without them?' He picked up his burger, lifted the top of the bun and waved it at her. 'Bread of enriched flour, four ounces of prime beef, lettuce, onion, tomato, pickle,' he enumerated. 'You have here, my dear, your fibre, your protein, your vitamins.' He looked meaningfully at the pale slice of half-ripe tomato decorating the burger amid the wash of ketchup and mustard.

'And your fat, your calories, your cholesterol and your salt,' she added helpfully.

He smiled indulgently. 'All of which are also essential to human nutrition. Don't be difficult, dear.'

He was in his playful mood; it wasn't difficult to recognize. But Megan wasn't going to be taken in by it. She remained coolly silent as she watched him take a hearty bite from his burger.

He made an inviting gesture, pointing out the other one. Then he frowned as he swallowed his food. 'You didn't turn into a health-food nut, did you?'

Despite herself, she smiled. 'No. Oh, what the hell!' She sat down and took the offered hamburger. It did look pretty good and she was starving.

'Good girl!'

'Oh, shut up!'

He grinned. 'Charming. You've grown some needles, I can tell.'

She ignored that, switched on the TV and settled back in her chair to eat and watch. He seemed content to do the same. She remembered how they used to watch TV, curled up on the couch together. The memory brought a stab of pain, and she got up quickly and went into the kitchen to make coffee. Oh, damn, damn! she thought. If I'm going to make this work, I'd better get myself under control. I can't let him get to me.

Nick was stretched out on the couch, hands behind his head, when she came back in the room with the coffee.

'Make yourself at home,' she said caustically, sorry the moment the words were out. She put the cups down, slopping coffee on to the table.

'Thank you,' he said evenly. He sat up and faced her. 'All right, let's talk.'

'About what?'

'About you and me.'

'You and me are a chapter that's closed as far as I'm concerned,' she shrugged.

'You're wrong. You and I are starting a brand-new chapter.'

She rolled her eyes. 'I'll do my job to the very best of my ability, don't worry, boss man.'

'And you don't think your hostility towards me will get in the way?' Nick picked up his cup and took a swallow, looking at her over the rim of the cup.

'Not as long as you can stay out of my personal life, and

stop barging into my house with a Burger King dinner.'

'It won't happen again. If my memory serves me, Burger King hasn't made it to Bali yet. However, if you have no objection to *ayam goreng* . . .'

He was taunting her, the glint of amusement in his eyes proof of that, but she refused to rise to the bait.

'I want you to listen to me,' she said. 'I want that job and I intend to do it right. I intend to have a civilised, professional relationship with you. I don't think anything else is called for.'

Nick nodded slowly, as if considering this. 'You're quite right. My only concern is that our past relationship might get in the way of our professionalism.'

'Not for me,' she snapped. 'Just keep out of my personal life.'

'That may be a problem on a small island like Bali,' he said with maddening calm. 'The foreign community is very small, so we'll be thrown together all the time. There's no avoiding it.' He sounded very reasonable.

Of course, what he said was true. There would be parties, sports events, meetings. Her contact with Nick would not be limited to the work situation only, she might as well accept that.

'We'll have to manage, somehow, won't we?' she asked coolly.

He gave her a long, searching look. 'Yes, we will. I just wanted to make sure you understood.'

'Oh, I understand.'

He drained his cup, came to his feet and picked up his coat. 'Thanks for the coffee.' He opened the door and hesitated for a moment, as if about to say something. He studied her face, and for a brief moment she recognised the look in his eyes and felt her heart contract. Then he looked away, and stepped out, wishing her goodnight.

After she had closed the door, Megan leaned against the

wall, her knees trembling.

She felt a terrible sense of doom.

Get out while you still can! her instinct warned. Call him tomorrow and call the whole thing off!

But, of course, she did not. Megan Opperman, after all, loved challenges and adventure. Megan Opperman was not a coward. Megan Opperman liked to live dangerously. Megan Opperman wanted to go to Bali.

She looked at herself in the bathroom mirror and grimaced.

Megan Opperman was probably stupid.

The next day she told Jason about the job on Bali, and about the possibility of her going there for two or three years. His face was impassive as he listened to her, his calm brown eyes betraying nothing.

'It's the perfect job for me, Jason. It's going to be great for my career.' Why did she feel she had to justify herself? Why did she feel guilty? There was no reason to. There were no promises, no commitments between them.

'Of course, I understand.' He turned a page in the newspaper and smiled. 'Let's hope it works out for you. Bali is supposed to be a wonderful place.' He went back to his reading, the paper hiding his face. Megan didn't know what to think. He certainly had taken the news with good grace. She should be relieved, yet she felt unaccountably irritated. She stared at the back of the paper, suppressing an urge to take it out of Jason's hands and shake him. Hey! Didn't you hear what I said? I'm leaving!

You know what's the matter with you? she asked herself. You had expected a more passionate response than that. In your heart of hearts you don't want him to be able to let you go quite that easily, as if you didn't matter to him. It hurts your vanity. You feel rejected. The thought almost made her laugh. After all, wasn't she the one doing the rejecting?

Wasn't she the one doing the leaving, the saying goodbye? She got up and went into the kitchen to make coffee.

What's the matter with you? she asked her reflection in the kitchen window. It's the way you wanted it, isn't it? No more commitments, no more emotional entanglements, no more tears and sleepless nights. You did that once, and never again. She closed her eyes briefly.

No, she thought fiercely, *never again!*

Six weeks later she received a phone call from CCD to inform her that they had been awarded the contract and preparations were being made for her and Nick's departure.

Megan handed in her resignation and started making lists—a shopping list and a things-to-do list. The days passed in a blur. There was so much to do and think about that every night she fell into bed exhausted, only to wake up three hours later with her mind full of details still to attend to. Her sleep was restless, filled with dread and trepidation. Part of her was convinced she was making the mistake of her life. Another part wouldn't admit it.

Nick called again. 'You have time for a drink tonight? Or better yet, dinner?'

'Why?'

'Business, of course.' His voice was dry. 'Don't sound so suspicious.'

Megan gritted her teeth. 'What do you want?'

'Dinner. Preferably something nice and expensive.'

'I mean, what's the business you want to discuss?'

He laughed. 'There's a slight change in plans. Nothing major. And I have some information about prefab housing from Australia I'd like you to see.'

'Prefab houses are a lousy idea.'

'Let's argue about it over dinner. I'll pick you up at your place at seven.'

'I don't want to . . .' She heard the click. She slammed the

phone down, cursing him under her breath. There were
ways to get out of tonight's dinner, of course. She could
simply refuse to go with him. Then he'd probably stay and
talk to her at home. She could go out earlier and not be
home at seven when he came to pick her up. Not very
professional, or mature.

The man wanted to talk business. In another week, he'd
be her boss. OK, she'd do the mature thing and be ready
when he came. Prefab housing, that was what he wanted to
discuss? Well, he'd better be ready to listen to her!

The restaurant was magnificent. Nick had even donned a
suit and tie for the occasion. He looked as if he never wore
anything else, the easy elegance completely natural. Nick
was one of those men who could wear anything, from the
most casual to the most formal, and look at ease in it. There
was a self-assuredness about him, a self-confidence that
carried through in every aspect of his life. He was at home
anywhere, never felt or looked out of place. It was part of
his male appeal, and Megan was very aware of it as they
followed the maître d' through the restaurant.

The décor was subtly classy, with a continental flair.
'Very impressive,' Megan commented after they had been
seated. 'But, for a business dinner, isn't this overdoing it a
bit?'

'I felt I had to make up for the lukewarm burgers I offered
you last time.'

'This will probably do it.'

They ordered drinks and discussed the menu. Everything
looked delicious. I might as well enjoy this, she said to
herself as she scanned the list.

'What kind of information about prefab houses did you
get from Australia?' she asked as soon as the waiter had
taken their orders.

'There's a company in Perth who'll work with our
designs, or modify their own existing designs. If we want

them to, they'll send out a crew to demonstrate and train local workmen.'

'It must be pretty expensive,' she commented. 'It makes much more sense to me to use local materials and build local types of houses.'

'Which will take ten times as long. These prefab jobs are put up in a couple of days.'

'If you know what you're doing. And if you're talking time, you have to think of how long it will take to get the materials in. Shipping can be a major headache, and believe me, I have experience with that.'

There were other points to discuss, and they went over them all through their dinner, which was as delicious as it had promised to be.

'We'll just have to wait and study the situation when we get to Bali,' said Nick at last. 'And that brings me to the other issue. There are several low-cost house projects on Java. What we'll do is fly to Jakarta and have the CCD office there give us a car. We'll drive the length of the island, visit the projects and see what we can learn. That'll take about a week. Then we'll take the ferry across to Bali.'

Megan slowly put her coffee-cup down. A week travelling through Java. A week alone in a car with Nick. Purgatory would be more fun!

'Whose idea was that?' she asked.

'Mine. I think it will be very helpful for both of us to have a look.'

There was no denying that. She didn't know what to say, but anger began to build inside her. *Damn, damn!* she thought. It's looking worse by the minute! I'm not supposed to have this job! She crumpled the napkin in her lap and pressed her lips together.

Nick looked into her eyes, his face inscrutable. 'I'm sorry if the idea of spending a week with me on the road doesn't appeal to you.'

'If it's necessary, it'll have to be done.'

'Thank you,' he said drily. 'And I'd like it if you didn't hate me quite so much.'

'This job is beginning to look like a nightmare,' Megan said to Christa as she put a bowl of soup in front of her on the low coffee-table. 'As if it isn't bad enough that he's my boss, now the two of us are driving across Java for a week, to look at some other low-cost housing projects.'

Christa pursed her lips thoughtfully. 'Sounds like a potentially . . . er . . . interesting situation.'

Megan grimaced and sat down, yoga style, on a cushion facing Christa. 'I'm tempted to forget the whole thing.'

'But it's the perfect job for you!'

'That's what I thought, too.' She stirred the steaming soup. 'God, how ironic!'

'Well, think of it this way,' said Christa. 'After a week in a car together, you'll have it all sorted out. Either you'll be the best of friends, or you will have killed each other off.'

'And there's always a plane back if it doesn't work.'

'Breach of contract doesn't do your career any good, though,' Christa pointed out.

'Quitting before I start won't do my pride any good.'

Christa blew in her soup. 'Pride is a dangerous emotion. They've fought wars because of pride.'

'Well, if you haven't got pride, what do you have?'

'How about common sense?'

Megan made a face. 'You weren't supposed to have an answer for that one.' She swallowed some soup. 'This stuff is revolting!'

'Did you make it?'

'Thanks a lot! Even I could do better than this. What do you suppose they put in it? Ground up worms? Cactus juice?'

'Heavens, no, nothing natural. Read the label.'

'I'm afraid to. Here, give me your bowl. I'll find us something else.'

'Why don't we order a pizza?'

'I'm sick of pizza. How about Chinese?'

'Fine. I know a place that delivers. Cute delivery boy, too. I'll call.'

They were in the middle of their Szechuan pork when the phone rang.

'Megan? This is Sam.'

'Sam?' she queried.

'Sam Stuart.'

'Oh! Yes, Sam, the almost-doctor.'

'I must have made a great impression on you,' Sam remarked ruefully.

'I repressed it.'

He laughed. 'Repression is dangerous. It can make you sick.'

'According to my friends, I already am.'

'Maybe I should make a house call.'

'It's against American Medical Association regulations.'

'How about Megan Opperman regulations?'

'Definitely against.'

He let out a sigh of defeat. 'I'll be in Washington next week. I was hoping to take you out to dinner.'

'I'm afraid you're out of luck.'

'The professor?' Sam asked.

'My reasons are my own.'

'How about if Christa comes along to chaperon?'

'No go.'

'How about if the professor joins us, too?' he persisted.

'No, thank you.'

'You're a tough lady.'

Megan made a face and glanced over at Christa. 'You've no idea how tough.'

* * *

'We've got your tickets and hotel reservations,' Nick was saying over the telephone. 'You want to pick them up here at the office, or shall I drop them off?'

'Why not put them in the mail?'

'Too risky, at this point in the game. If you prefer to get them here, come by tomorrow some time.'

Megan couldn't make it, the packers were coming. A friend was coming over tomorrow to take over the lease on the apartment. There were a hundred other things to do. She sighed.

'I can't get away. Drop them off, then, if you don't mind.'

'I don't mind, or I wouldn't have offered. I'll be by later this evening. Around nine.'

She was drinking coffee and sorting out a stack of paperbacks when he arrived. The place looked bare with all her pictures gone and the rugs rolled up. Most of her belongings would go into storage. Some things would be sent to Bali by airfreight, some by boat.

It was just after nine when Nick arrived.

'You're making progress,' he said, looking around. 'I haven't had time to start yet.' He took a bundle of papers from his inner coat pocket. 'Here you go. Make sure you check them to see they're all in order.'

'It's not my first trip overseas, Nick. Stop treating me like a schoolgirl!' she protested.

He frowned. 'Sorry.' He rubbed his forehead. 'By the way, we won't be travelling together. I have to go to Hong Kong to see someone. I'll meet you at the hotel in Jakarta.'

Good, great! She hadn't looked forward to spending thirty-odd hours in the small confines of an aeroplane with him. 'All right,' she agreed.

'You don't seem overly distressed,' he said drily.

'I'm not.'

He rubbed his forehead again. 'Do you have some aspirin? I've got a raging headache, and I won't be home for a couple of hours yet.'

'Sure. I'll get them.' She extracted herself from the piles of books and got up. 'Sit down. I'll be right back.'

She gave him a couple of tablets, dropping them in his hand without touching it, then handed him a glass of water. 'How about some coffee? Sometimes that helps. It contracts the blood vessels in the brain, or expands them, I don't remember which.'

Nick's smile was faintly amused. 'It's worth a try.' He put the aspirin in his mouth and downed the water.

When she came back with the coffee, he had taken off his coat and was looking through one of her books. *How to Talk to Your Pig,* the title read.

'Is this yours?' he asked, eyebrows raised.

Morgan shrugged. 'I haven't the foggiest idea how it got here. I've never owned a pig.' She put the cups on the table.

'But if you did you'd probably talk to it.'

She gave him a challenging look. 'Probably.'

'You may have your chance yet. Lots of pigs on Bali. Maybe you can get yourself one as a pet.'

'Bali pigs are ugly as sin. The cows are cute, though.'

'Cute? Cows?' Nick's laugh was low and amused.

She sipped her coffee. 'Yes, cute,' she said with a straight face. 'Small and brown, like little Jerseys, and very gentle. At least, they look it.'

'I've seen them. I wouldn't call them cute, though, but I can see why you would.'

She decided not to pursue that. 'Have you heard anything about our housing yet?' she asked.

He nodded. 'Finally. A house for you and a house for me, and an office in the district government building. I got a telegram today. The houses are supposed to be fully furnished—tables, chairs, beds, kitchen stove and refrigerator.'

'Good. I was beginning to wonder if we'd have to camp

out under the coconut palms once we got there.'

'Might be interesting, actually. But everything seems to be taken care of. So far, so good.' Nick took another swallow of his coffee and looked at her. 'There's something else I wanted to tell you. I've decided that you were right about those prefab houses from Australia.'

'You have?' Surprise coloured her voice.

His mouth quirked. 'I have. How about that? Me big injun chief wrong. You little squaw right.'

'And you even admit it. Miracles never cease!'

'Now, now don't be nasty!' Nick drained his cup and put it on the table. 'I checked the shipping route. They couldn't bring the materials straight to Bali. The shipment would go to Singapore first, or maybe Jakarta. Then it would all have to be reloaded on to smaller boats to come to Bali. It would take too much time and trouble. Secondly, I did some figuring and it's too expensive, like you said.'

Megan couldn't help but feel a sense of triumph. 'I'm glad. That's one thing we don't have to argue about any more.'

He got up and put his trench coat on again. 'I'd prefer it if we didn't have to argue about anything, but that would be too much to hope for, I suppose.'

She nodded and came to her feet. 'Probably.'

He looked at her for a quiet moment. 'Thanks for the TLC,' he said softly.

'You're welcome.'

He smiled, and she felt herself grow warm under the blue gaze. Then he reached out, took her face between his hands and his mouth touched hers, his lips warm and firm on hers in a quick yet oddly tender kiss.

'Goodnight, Megan. I'll see you in Jakarta.'

She leaned against the wall, her heart racing. She stared at the closed door, thinking how easy it had once been to love him, how little she had ever understood him, and wondered how she was going to manage working with him for the next couple of years.

Jason became quieter and quieter in the last weeks before her departure. Megan had not expected him to take her leaving so badly. Had she misjudged him, after all? His morose silences began to grate on her nerves, and at the same time a vague sense of guilt clouded her mind.

'Dammit!' Jason exploded one night. 'All you think and talk about is that job and your career! So what about me?'

'I made no promises, Jason.' Megan spoke quietly, not wanting to make a public display in the restaurant where they were having their meal.

'I'm not talking about promises, I'm talking about feelings! Don't you feel anything for me?'

'Of course I do. You know that.'

'But not enought to stay here.' Plea and accusation mingled in his tone. His eyes were dark and stormy. He picked up his wine and took a long gulp.

She'd never seen him quite so agitated. She put her fork down; the *linguini* Alfredo she'd craved all afternoon had suddenly lost its appeal. 'I've got to think about my career, Jason. I thought you understood that.'

He closed his eyes. 'I do, intellectually.'

She looked at his hand on the table, the long fingers turned under, as if unconsciously trying to hold on to something.

'Jason,' she said gently, 'you know as well as I do that our relationship isn't going anywhere. You even *wanted* it that way yourself. You kept telling me that in the beginning, don't you remember? You didn't *want* any ties, any promises.'

And that had been fine with her. She didn't want any, either. She and Jason understood each other. It was comfortable, pleasant, convenient. There was always someone to have a meal with, to take to a party, to go see a new play with. There were no expectations, no commitments. There was no love.

He'd come out of a bad marriage only months before they met, and a new commitment was the last thing he wanted. She'd never asked him about his wife or their marriage, and he had never told her. She didn't want to know. The less she knew, the better. There was very little she had ever told him about herself, and he had not asked.

It had been so different with Nick. Nick had known everything about her—her life in small-town Maine, the loss of her father, her most embarrassing moment in school, her dog, her first date. And she'd known everything about him—where he'd gone to school, the things he did as a child, his family background. She'd met his father, had looked at his boyhood photo albums.

Jason looked gloomily at his spinach soufflé. 'I didn't expect to get so attached to you,' he sighed.

Attached. Like a dog, Megan thought wryly. Pleasant, comfortable. She closed her eyes briefly. 'I'm sorry, Jason.'

He raised his eyebrows. 'You are?'

She nodded. 'Of course I am! I didn't mean for either one of us to get hurt! We'd even set it up so we wouldn't.'

'I guess you can't regulate your emotions,' he said ruefully. 'Maybe it's one of the mistakes I made—thinking I had control over them.'

'Jason, please don't make more out of this than there is,' she begged.

'What do you mean?'

'Don't tell yourself you love me.' Her toes curled in her shoes. 'Because it isn't true, Jason.' Whatever his feelings for her, it wasn't love. He didn't love her. She didn't love him. The only man she'd ever loved was Nick.

She did not see Jason again before she left. He sent her a box of books, with a note wishing her success in her career

and happiness in her life. The night before her departure
she tried to call him, but he wasn't home.

The taxi ride to the Borobudur Hotel in Jakarta was hair-
raising. The streets teemed with a variety of
vehicles—three-wheeled motor-cycle cabbies, fume-spewing
buses, dilapidated trucks, motor-cycles—all racing down the
road as if they had it to themselves. The taxi was well
beyond retirement age, but somehow still smoked and
sputtered through the traffic at death-defying speed. No air-
conditioning. No meter.

Perspiration ran down Megan's back and her dress clung
damply to her skin. She wound down the window to catch a
little breeze on her face. The air was thick with fumes and
gases and the smells of sewers, rotting garbage and general
decay.

The hotel was like another world. Luxurious,
sumptuous—a cool, clean oasis in the torrid heat of the
odorous, sprawling city of seven million. It was a self-
contained world, with a shopping arcade, several
restaurants and bars, meeting rooms, offices, a health club,
parklike grounds with tennis courts, a jogging track, a mini
golf course and a huge, sparkling swimming pool with its
own outside restaurant.

She checked in and was taken to her room. Plush
carpeting, a gleaming bathroom, a king-size bed. From the
window, she had a view over the Kintamani gardens, the
palms, the blooming bougainvillaea, the blue, blue pool. It
looked very inviting. Beyond lay the city, with its tall,
colourless buildings towering over the smaller houses with
their smudgy red-tiled roofs, bathing in a smoky haze of
pollution.

Megan was exhausted from her long plane trip, but a dip
in the pool before crashing on the bed didn't seem like a bad
idea. It would be her last day alone, and she'd better make

the most of it. Tomorrow Nick would arrive and work would begin. She felt a tightening in her stomach just at the thought of it. Panic hovered on the edges of her consciousness and was never far away. She forced it down, determined not to give in to it.

She fished her bikini from her suitcase, had a quick shower and put it on. She didn't have much of a tan any more; the one she'd acquired in the Caribbean was long gone. She examined her pale reflection. The bikini was black, which made her look even paler. Well, it wouldn't last long. On Bali she could even go topless if she had the guts. She probably wouldn't. From her former visit to the island she knew that her puritanical American instincts were firmly embedded. The European and Aussie tourists who swarmed all over the beaches seemed to have no such hang-ups.

Only three people were in the pool, and it was a glorious feeling to have the space to swim a couple of slow, easy laps and to get her stiff and cramped muscles loosened up again. She climbed out, got a cold orange juice from the refreshment stand and settled on a lounger to dry.

In the shade, the temperature was perfect. She sipped her drink contentedly, surveying her surroundings. All around the pool, tropical plants and trees grew luxuriantly: scarlet hibiscus, creamy white and yellow frangipani, majestic palms. An open restaurant with a thatched roof flanked one side. A cart for cold drinks was close at hand. And all she had to do was lie here and relax. This was the life! With a little bit of imagination, she could pretend to be leading the jet-set life of a swinging single. She grinned at herself.

'Hello, Megan.'

Her heart lurched at the sound of the familiar voice. She opened her eyes. Nick. His body, still so familiar, was right there in front of her, clad in nothing but short blue swimming trunks. Wide shoulders, broad chest with the dark, curly hair, narrow hips and long muscular legs. The body she had once loved so much. She stared at him, speechless with a sudden primitive yearning.

Oh, God, she thought, closing her eyes again, this is not what I need right now.

CHAPTER THREE

'I THOUGHT you weren't going to be here until tomorrow.' Megan's body was rigid and the tension in her voice did not go unnoticed.

Hands on his hips, blue eyes amused, Nick looked down at her with a faint smile. 'I'm sorry to disappoint you—change of schedule. The guy I was seeing in Hong Kong was in a car accident and is comatose in the hospital. I thought I might as well come straight down. How's the water?'

'Fine,' she said curtly.

'Room all right?'

'Very comfortable, thanks. I didn't know CCD treated its staff to five-star hotels.'

'I pulled a few strings,' Nick explained.

'Mmm.' She closed her eyes against the glare of the sun and against the glare of Nick's bodily perfection. It called up too many memories, too many needs and desires she didn't want to feel.

'Where would you like to have dinner tonight?' he asked.

Megan hadn't even thought of dinner. She wasn't hungry. 'I don't want any. I'm going up now to crash. If I'm hungry when I wake up, I'll order something from room service.' She came to her feet and picked up her towel. She could feel his eyes on her like a physical touch, and felt naked under his regard. It made her angry and defensive. Damn the man! Did he have to look at her like that?

His gaze returned to her face. 'You'd do better not to sleep too long. Have a rest and then go on with the day. Helps your biological clock adjust itself.'

She tried hard to control her irritation. 'It's not the first time I've dealt with jet lag, Nick.' She slipped her feet into her white leather thongs. 'I'll see you tomorrow some time.'

He made no reply and she walked away, feeling his eyes following her the whole length of the pool.

In her dreams, Megan heard him calling her name.

'Go away,' she called. 'Go away!' I don't want you any more, don't you understand? So don't stand there and look at me with those laughing eyes. I don't want you any more!

There was a loud knocking, filling her dream, her room. She moaned, turning in the bed, half-conscious.

'Megan! Open the door.'

She opened her eyes, suddenly awake, the knocking on the door pounding in her head. She swung her legs over the edge of the bed, picked up a towel and wrapped it around herself. Stumbling to the door, she opened it.

'What the hell do you think you're doing?' she demanded.

'Trying to wake you up.' Nick pushed past her into the room, carrying a tray with two cups of coffee.

'Get out of my room!'

'Don't make a scene, Meggie,' he said soothingly, setting the tray on the table and pushing the door shut. 'I told you, you can adjust yourself to the local time better if you have dinner at a normal time and then go to bed at the regular time tonight. The sooner you're over jet lag, the better. We have a lot of travelling to do in the next few days.' He smiled at her charmingly. 'Here, a cup of coffee to wake you up.'

Megan stared at him, open-mouthed. 'I can't believe this,' she said on a low note. 'The gall—the audacity! You're my boss, not my caretaker! I'm perfectly capable of deciding for myself how to deal with my jet lag!"

Nick shrugged, unconcerned, his smile not fading. 'Actually, I had an ulterior motive. I hate to have dinner alone in hotel restaurants. You know how it is. So boring not to have anyone to discuss the wine with, so lonely to see all those other happy couples enjoying themselves and . . .'

'My heart bleeds for you! Now get out!'

'Oh, come on now, be a sport. Have your coffee, have a shower, and let's go.'

'Go to hell!'

'Later.' He took her arm, propelled her into the bathroom and, still holding her with one hand, turned on the shower. Then he took hold of the towel and whipped it away from her.

Megan was too outraged to speak. He smiled down at her.

'Get in,' he ordered.

'No!'

His hands began to move up her arms to her face.

'Take your hands off me!' she hissed. In the small room, she had no place to go. He had her trapped firmly between his body and the tub.

'You're just the way I remember you,' he said softly, his eyes sliding over her naked body.

Pain mingled with the fury. 'Bastard!'

He shook his head. 'No, Megan.' There was an odd tone to his voice, and suddenly his mouth covered hers and he pressed her close against him.

A convulsive tremor ran through her. Oh, God, she thought, not this, not this! A wave of pain and hot desire washed over her, drowning her, paralysing her. All the long-buried memories came rushing back. Helpless, she stood in his embrace, feeling his hands sliding over her body, the warmth of his mouth kissing her, tantalising her until her lips parted of their own accord.

This was the man who had shared her life for eighteen months, whose hands knew every inch of her body, every special, secret place, more than any other man had ever known. The man who had left her unexpectedly one soft September eve.

Suddenly Nick let go and leaned back against the door,

breathing hard. She noticed his hands, clenched into fists, the knuckles white. For a moment, words would not form in her mouth. She stared at him in a terrible mixture of silent rage and utter misery.

'Don't ever do that again!' she said in a low voice. 'Don't you *ever* do that again, or I'll swear to God I'll be on the next plane home!'

He flexed his fingers, then raked them through his hair. 'I always did like kissing you, Megan.' There was a hint of amusement in his tone now. 'And you always seemed to enjoy it. I'm sorry if I've lost my touch.'

He hadn't, and he knew it.

'What the hell is the matter with you?' she said fiercely, taking a towel to cover herself. 'Can't you keep your animal urges under control?'

'I guess not.'

'What's the matter? Didn't anybody want you after you had had enough of me?' A face flashed in her memory—Maxie Godwin. Didn't he want her, either?

'Actually, yes, a few did want me. I just didn't want them.'

'I should have guessed. None of them good enough for you, I imagine.'

He looked at her without answering. The small room was filling up with steam from the warm water, making her skin feel damp and slippery. It seemed to fill her head, her mind, her lungs, like the feeling of his presence, the oppresive closeness of him, the tension between them.

'Let me make one thing perfectly clear,' she said at last, clutching the towel to her. 'There may have been a time when we knew each other well, when we were on terms familiar enough to share a bed and a bathroom. But that time is in the past, and you have no right to similar privileges now. No right to come into my room when I'm not dressed. No right to stand there and look at me without my clothes on. You will have to respect my privacy. You employed me, you're my boss, and that's where it all stops.' She glared at him with all the fury of her determination.

'I'm sorry,' said Nick after a silence. He turned, walked out and closed the bathroom door quietly behind him.

Megan pushed the shower curtain aside and stepped in over the edge of the tub. Her whole body was trembling, and she closed her eyes and tried to douse her feelings with the water as it streamed over her. The tension in her broke suddenly. Tears mingled with the water and her body shook with her sobs.

Two years had not been enough to eradicate him from her mind and memory. She had only been pretending, repressing her feelings, hidng them. They were still there. Yet, after the pain he had caused her, she could never trust him again. She certainly didn't trust him now.

The tears kept coming, and she did not try to stop them, the build-up of memories too strong to fight. When it was over, she felt exhausted, yet relieved and curiously strong.

Nick was gone when she came back into the bedroom, but she found a note on the dressing-table. 'Please have dinner with me. Meet me at the Toba Rotisserie downstairs at eight. Nick.'

The gall of the man! Megan wadded up the paper and tossed it into the waste-paper basket with a well-aimed shot. Did he really think that all he had to do was say please and she'd come running? Did he really think she'd let him push her around? Well, he could forget it! 'No go, Mr Donovan,' she muttered out loud. 'I'll do as I please, and having dinner with you is not on the programme.'

She lay on the bed and read a paperback, but it was a struggle to keep her attention focused on it. After a while, she began to feel hungry and ordered something to eat from room service. While she ate, she watched an Indonesian news broadcast on TV, understanding next to nothing. It was depressing. Being alone in a hotel room was depressing. Having nobody to talk to was depressing. She spent another hour watching a bad video, then gave up and went to sleep.

The next morning, Nick did not mention her not showing up at the restaurant. They took a taxi to the CCD office and spent some time getting acquainted with the people and getting organised for their trip the next day. A car was ready for them, a Mitsubishi van in excellent condition.

Nick was in his business mode all day, which was a relief. They returned to the hotel in the middle of the afternoon. Megan was looking forward to a cool swim and a long drink.

'Do you have any plans for dinner tonight?' he asked, as they waited for their room keys at the desk. His voice was perfectly casual, the cool blue eyes betraying nothing but a polite interest.

'No,' she heard herself say, taking the key from the receptionist.

'Will you have dinner with me?'

Megan studied him for a moment, looking into the clear blue eyes, wondering what was going on in his mind. He didn't look exactly humble, but then he wasn't the humble type. 'All right,' she said at last.

'Good. I'll come and get you at eight.'

She was ready when he knocked, and she saw the surprise and admiration in the narrowing of his eyes as his gaze travelled over her.

She was all chic elegance in the pale green silk dress. Long silver ear-rings and high-heeled strappy shoes completed the outfit. Her stylish clothes gave her straight, sleek hairstyle a look of sophisticated simplicity. She didn't look like the Megan he knew, and she was quite aware of that as she watched him examine her.

'You look . . . beautiful,' he told her.

'Thank you.' He didn't look too bad himself. He was dressed in a casual lightweight suit, with an open-necked shirt underneath. He wore his clothes with comfortable ease, moving with the grace of an athlete. His hair was combed away from his forehead, and still slightly damp from his shower. He was a good-looking man. And there are thousands of other good-looking men, she amended. But he's just my boss and I'm going to work with him and that's that.

She picked up her room key and the small silver clutch bag and looked at him coolly. 'I'm ready.'

They did not venture out into town, but went to one of the hotel restaurants, a sumptuous place with soft lighting, white tablecloths and gleaming silverware. A single white orchid graced the table.

'A drink?' asked Nick.

'A sherry, please.'

'Medium dry?' Nick's mouth quirked. 'I'm learning.'

Megan examined the menu, not commenting. She didn't care if he learned or not. It was important not to care what Nick said or did. Once, she had cared too much. Everything was different now. A new game with new rules. And she was going to play it cool.

'So, what else will I have to learn about you?' he asked after the drinks had arrived.

Megan's shrug was casual. 'I have no idea.'

'You seem so different—very cool, very sophisticated. Not like I remember you at all.'

'Does that bother you?' she asked.

'No. It intrigues me.'

'Is that why we had that little charade in the bathroom yesterday. You wanted to see what was still left of that besotted little thing I once was?'

His mouth curled into a smile. 'Maybe.'

'Well, let me tell you. I don't appreciate little experiments of that nature,' Megan assured him.

Nick picked up his menu. 'I got that impression,' he said drily.

She felt the heat of anger rise inside her again. 'I don't know what kind of game you're playing, Nick, but whatever it is I'm not interested.'

'Stubborn as ever. At least that hasn't changed.'

She gritted her teeth and didn't answer. When the waiter came, she gave him her order and handed back the menu. Nick produced a map of the island of Java.

'We'll start as early as we can tomorrow morning. This is the itinerary. Ever been around Java?'

'No.' She looked at the map, her eyes following the red lines Nick had drawn across the length of the island.

'The scenery is spectacular. It's very densely populated, though, and people will be all over us. The Javanese are very friendly, very helpful. It'll be a good trip.'

She certainly hoped so. She sipped her sherry as he pointed out the various places they would visit, watching his hand as it moved across the map. He had good hands—large, capable, with a sprinkling of dark hair on the top and neat, square nails. She'd always liked his hands, the warm, solid grasp of them as they held hers, the feel of them against her skin. She closed her eyes briefly. Stop it, you fool. She opened her eyes, looking right into Nick's.

'Are you all right?'

'Of course I'm all right,' she said irritably, looking back down at the map.

He straightened and leaned back in his chair. 'I'm afraid I don't know about the accommodation. We may have to rough it a bit.' He gave her a quick, appraising glance. 'I assume, in your various wanderings, you've managed to survive less than luxurious sleeping arrangements?'

Megan raised a mocking eyebrow. 'Yes. I don't scream at the sight of a cockroach on the floor or a lizard on the ceiling.'

'You wouldn't think that, looking at you.'

She knew what he meant. Dressed like she was, she looked as if she'd led a life of leisure and luxury, and wasn't used to anything but the best. But the best wasn't always what you got when you travelled in Africa or other parts of the world. She'd seen her share of shabby hotels and dirty restaurants. He didn't have a think to worry about.

They discussed the trip while they ate, Megan carefully keeping everything she said businesslike and impersonal. She was aware of Nick's eyes looking at her with surprise and amazement at times, but she pretended not to notice. There was no doubt that he was puzzled by her behaviour.

After they'd left the restaurant, they strolled through the shopping arcade and looked at the display of batik paintings that hung along the upper gallery.

'Would you like to go outside and explore the gardens?' Nick asked as they reached the bank of escalators near the front entrance.

She stared at him. Did she want to come with him out into the night, and take a moonlight stroll through the tropical Kintamani Gardens? He had to be kidding! No way!

'No, thanks. I'm going up.'

A smile tugged at the corners of his mouth as he looked down at her. 'You used to like evening walks.'

'I used to like a lot of things,' she said coolly. A lot of things you didn't care about, she added silently.

'A changed woman!' he mocked. 'It should be an interesting trip.'

She ignored his taunt and turned away. 'Goodnight.'

'Megan?'

She looked back over her shoulder, impatient. 'What?'

There was a devilish gleam in his eyes. 'Would you like me to come and tuck you in after I come back?'

She gave him a withering look. 'Get lost!'

Nick laughed. 'I think I'll do that. I'll see you in the morning.'

'If I don't catch a plane home tonight,' muttered Megan under her breath.

'What?'

'Nothing.' She walked off. He was trying to get under her

skin, and she had no idea why. Of course, Nick had always relished challenges, and the idea of a woman not falling for his male charms was probably not easy to for his ego to digest. Even if that woman was one he'd dumped himself some years ago.

She'd given him everything then; and he hadn't wanted it. She had nothing for him now.

She took the elevator to her floor, sharing it with a young Indonesian couple holding hands and whispering to each other. The girl was elegantly dressed in the latest Javanese fashion, her black hair a mass of shiny curls around her head. The elevator stopped and Megan got out. Her room was the last one on the floor, and as she walked along the long, straight corridor she could not escape the thought that she was fleeing from Nick, from the haunting memories that wouldn't let themselves stay buried. Deep down, she was frightened, scrambling frantically to build up a defensive wall to hide behind.

She let herself in and locked and chained the door. Inelegantly, she plopped herself down on the side of the bed, kicked off her heels and picked up the phone. She looked for the number and dialled.

'Room service. May I help you?' The language of the hotel was English, which was a relief. Megan had spent some time with books and tapes, trying to learn the rudimentaries of Indonesian, but had so far not mastered much.

'I'd like a cup of tea, please. No milk, no sugar.'

She undressed, took off her make-up and got ready for bed. When the tea came, she took a book and slid between the cool sheets of the big bed. Her bed-time ritual had not changed over the years—sipping tea and reading before going to sleep. But that was one thing Nick wasn't likely to find out. She remembered how he had liked to tease her about drinking tea in bed.

'You and your tea,' he'd say, shaking his head, smiling.

'What if you run out?'

'I make sure I don't.' Even on her trips she'd carry tea with her. A cup of hot water was always available, wherever she was.

'And if you don't, you can't sleep. There's caffeine in tea, for heaven's sake!'

'It doesn't bother me. I'm used to it. The day isn't finished right if I don't have tea—it's just a habit. It relaxes me. And I have the right to my little oddities.'

'You certainly do,' Nick said indulgently. 'At least it's innocent.'

'Right. It could be Scotch.'

'Now, *that* I could understand.'

She made a face. 'I'm a tea person, not a boozer. Sorry to disappoint you.'

'You don't disappoint me. You amuse me.'

Often the tea would grow cold by the bed, forgotten in the delights of lovemaking.

'Would you like me to get you another cup?' Nick would whisper in her ear as they lay curled up together afterwards, languid and content, his fingers playing with a long thick strand of her hair.

'No, don't go.' And she'd hold on to him, burying her face in his neck, smelling the warm, male scent of him, knowing she'd never want any man but him.

'What if you can't sleep?'

'With you here, I don't care.'

Her book slid off the bed. She stared at the gold and black cover unseeingly, as it gleamed up at her accusingly from the floor. For a moment she closed her eyes tightly, forcing her mind to go blank. Memories could be terrible things. She picked up the cup next to her bed and sipped the tea.

It was cold.

The Mitsubishi van jerked, then swerved sideways, and with a curse Nick applied the brakes and came to a standstill by the side of the road.

'What's wrong?'

'A flat tyre.' He opened the door and jumped out. Megan followed him, seeing the ruined tyre on her side as soon as she got out. They were on a straight stretch of road, heavily wooded on one side, and overlooking the hills, with rice paddies, on the other.

Nick kicked the tyre. 'Oh, hell!' Then he let out a heavy sigh of resignation. 'All right, give me a hand, will you?'

'Me? I don't know a thing about changing tyres.'

His eyebrows rose. 'You don't know how to change a tyre?' His tone of voice held a wealth of meaning.

Megan gave him a haughty look. 'No.'

He put his hands on his hips and surveyed her with mocking amusement. 'Here you are, a career woman in the eighties, and you don't know how to change a tyre?'

'Right again! Very good!' She leaned casually against the car and looked straight into his eyes, daring him to make anyting of it.

'And what would you do if you ever ended up with one?'

She shrugged lightly. 'It hasn't happened so far. But, if it did, I'd probably stand by the road, hitch up my skirt and wait for Robert Redford to come by.'

'Yeah, that figures.'

She deserved that, she had to admit. She had never had any desire to learn anything about cars. Mechanics did not interest her. It probably wasn't smart, though, not to know the basics of car maintenance. She'd meant to take a course for some time now, but had never actually enrolled. There'd always been handy excuses—too much work, a trip, something. Anyway, so far she'd been lucky.

He turned and fished out the jack from a space under the seat. 'Go find me the damn spare!' he ordered.

'Where is it?'

'I don't know! Just look!'

'You mean to say, you didn't check we actually had one before we left?'

'No.' He glowered at her. 'You want to make something of it?'

She smiled sweetly. 'Yes, I do. Not very smart, is it? We may not have one. Or it may be flat, too. You're a good one to criticise!'

Without answering, he opened the back, found the spare and lifted it out. It was in fine shape. Of course, it would be, she thought nastily. He began to jack up the car.

'Come over here and watch. You might as well learn something.'

'Why?' She didn't know what made her act like that, take some sort of perverse pleasure in taunting him.

'I don't think you can count on Robert Redford in the wilds of Java.'

She sauntered over to him. 'You think it's pretty dumb I don't know how to do this, right?'

'Right.'

'Do you know how to sew on a button and fix a split seam?' she challenged.

He looked up and gave a crooked grin. 'I do, sweetheart, I do.'

'Well, that's more than you knew two years ago.'

'That's more than you *assumed* I knew two years ago.' He began to twist off the bolts.

'And what do you mean by that?'

'Exactly what I said. You were always so eager to do everything for me, I never got a chance.' His voice was even, but the words hit her with needle precision.

You were always so eager to do everything for me . . . She had been, hadn't she? All she had ever wanted was to please him, make him happy, love him.

Her heart contracted. And you didn't want that, she

returned silently. 'You didn't want me doing things for you, loving you. Why did you never tell me?'

A lump formed in her throat and she turned away, noticing a group of small children staring at them. A little girl, not older than four or five, carried a small baby in a sling on her back. She was barefoot and the faded dress was too big for her and ripped in the front. The children looked on silently, their dark eyes solemn, as Nick picked up the spare tyre and proceeded to put it in place.

Megan got her camera from the car, smiled at the children, then pointed at the Pentax. *'Bisa* photo?' she asked.

They giggled and nodded. *'Bisa,'* the older girl agreed.

She took several pictures, some close-ups, then put the camera away. *'Terimah kasih,'* she thanked them.

She wondered where they had come from so suddenly. She saw no village, no houses anywhere, only the vista of jewel-green rice paddies curving along the hillside. The view was even more spectacular than the pictures she'd seen. There was a serene, artistic quality to the patterned green landscape, undulating under the azure sky.

She stood in the shade, watching the children watch Nick. It didn't take him long to attach the spare, and moments later he tossed the bad tyre in the back and put away the jack and wrench.

'Bring me the water,' he ordered, rubbing his dirty hands with a rag he'd found in the car.

'It's drinking water.' They had a big Thermos, filled at the hotel that morning, but they'd already drunk most of it.

'I'll just have to use some of it.'

'There isn't much left! What are we going to do when it's gone?'

He gave her a long-suffering look. 'This isn't the Sahara, for Pete's sake! We'll find something else to drink. Now, are you going to get me the water, or what?'

She gritted her teeth, got the bottle, opened it and poured

some over his hands.

'More!'

She poured more. The children inched closer and giggled. Several more had joined them and they stood around in a semicircle, fascinated by the sight of the tall foreigner washing his hands.

Nick grinned at them. *'Selamat sore,'* he greeted them.

'Selamat sore,' came the chorus of voices. More giggles. Their eyes were alight with curiosity.

Nick dried his hands and tossed the rag back in the car. 'Well, I guess this will have to do.'

They got back in their seats. Nick started the engine and the children waved and shrieked greetings as they drove off.

'Where did they all come from?' asked Megan, straightening the skirt of her yellow cotton dress.

He shrugged. 'Out of the woodwork. There are houses and *kampongs* everywhere, but you don't always see them. On Java, you're never alone.'

It was silent for a long time. They had been on the road since early that morning, and it had not been an easy day. The traffic was heavy on the narrow, winding roads, and the heat suffocating. There was no air-conditioning in the Mitsubishi. The car was about a year old. Once in Bali, they would get another car, one with air-conditioning if Megan had her way.

As was the custom in Indonesia, a driver had been allocated along with the car, but Nick had not wanted to take him on, preferring to do the driving himself. He had also refused Megan's offer to share the driving, with the argument that she wasn't used to driving on the left and that a main road in Java was not the place to start practising. She had to agree, he was right. The traffic frightened her senseless, but she hadn't wanted to admit it. It would be easier to get used to driving on Bali.

Megan stared outside, taking in the scenery, examining the clusters of small houses in the villages they passed through.

Cement and brick structures mingled with the traditional houses made of wood and bamboo with thatched palm-frond roofs.

Apparently the Javanese had a love for colour, because many of the small houses were painted bright blue, green, turquoise, pink or even violet, and often a combination of two or three of these. Chickens, goats and dogs wandered freely among the houses and children played in the swept dirt underneath the tall coconut palms that shaded the houses.

How different this looked from the place where she had grown up—a suburban home with a green lawn and a swing set in the backyard. No palm trees, but low evergreen bushes flanking the house, and azaleas that flowered in the spring. No dirt roads, but a tar-topped driveway coming off a wide paved street. For Nick, it had not been much different, although the house he had grown up in was much larger and set in an acre of beautifully landscaped grounds. His father had done well for himself and his family.

Poor Mr Donovan! Only one son and he didn't want to take over his company. Nick had never been interested in the furniture business. His interests had gone further and wider. Megan glanced over at Nick.

'Did you see your father before you left?'

His jaw went rigid. 'Yes.' His tone of voice gave a clear indication that he was not willing to discuss the subject.

Megan had met his father only a few times, and she'd liked the old man, respecting him for what he had accomplished. Yet she certainly didn't blame Nick for wanting to go his own way. But it had always bothered her that there was so much rancour and bitterness between father and son, maybe because she had lost her own father when she was only nine and would have paid any price to have him back, to have him love her again, to talk to him—just to have him in her life.

She had tried, in her own way, to bring peace between father and son, to make Nick more tolerant of his father's shortcomings, to make him understand his point of view and accept him for what he was. But every effort on her part had been met with resistance and resentment. 'My father is *my* problem,' he'd once exploded with furious finality, and after that she'd not dared mention the subject again.

Judging by the hard line of his jaw and mouth, the problem was still there.

She looked outside, saying no more.

'There's a small town coming up,' Nick said some time later. 'We'll stop and have a drink.'

They'd had their lunch in the car: sandwiches and fruit prepared for them by the hotel. They had had a long day ahead of them, and Nick had decided to take food along to save time.

Megan looked at the map spread out on her lap. In actual miles, they hadn't come that far today. But driving was difficult on the narrow curving roads, and the traffic of buses and trucks and ox-carts was a colourful, sometimes heart-stopping spectacle of risks.

Nick stopped at a small open-air restaurant on the main road through the town. A few small square tables stood neatly arranged under the metal roof, and each held small bottles of soy sauce and hot pepper sauce.

Nick looked at her questioningly. 'Coke? Orange Fanta?'

'Just some bottled water, please.' Megan had found on Java that the soft drinks were unbearably sweet, much more so than at home, to accommodate the sweet tooth of the Indonesians.

A handsome young boy, in tight trousers and a clean white T-shirt, took their order and was back moments later with their drinks and glasses filled with ice. He began to open the bottles. Megan looked suspiciously at the ice, wondering if it was made of safe drinking water.

'Should I use the ice?'

Nick shrugged. 'It's probably all right, but to be on the safe side I'd drink it straight from the bottle.'

She took the bottle from the kid before he had a chance to pour it into the glass and smiled. 'It's all right, thank you—*terimah kasih*.'

The bottle had not been refrigerated, and the water was lukewarm. Megan looked longingly at the ice, but resisted the temptation. Nick drank his warm beer without comment, long legs stretched out in front of him. He looked tired. His hair had fallen over his forehead again and she noticed small lines edging his mouth. For one crazy moment, she felt the urge to brush his hair back, to touch his mouth with her fingers and make the tiredness fade away in a smile. She looked away, taking a drink from the bottle.

It didn't take long before the first diminutive entrepreneur spotted them. He was about eight, and carried a stack of newspapers. Nick have him a coin and told him to get lost. Next was a kid who wanted to shine their shoes. Nick politely refused, then caved in with a sigh when the boy wouldn't take no for an answer. Number three peddled street maps of the town. Nick bought one.

Megan watched the procedures with growing amusement. Seeing this soft side of Nick was an unexpected treat. She shook her head at him and smiled. 'God, you're a sucker! I can't believe it.'

He glowered at her as he swallowed the last of his beer. 'Drink up and let's let out of here. These guys have some internal radar. They spot a pale face a mile away.'

They reached Cilicap at dusk, and found a small hotel on the main road. It was an old colonial structure, painted white, with ornate gables and wrought-iron gates. Despite its slightly dilapidated appearance, the building had character.

'What do you think?' Nick asked as they were shown their rooms by the dignified old proprietor, who was dressed in a sarong, long-sleeved batik shirt, and black pill-box hat.

'It's fine.' Megan looked around the small room. The linoleum was worn, the furniture old and sparse—a bed with a sagging mattress, a chair and a small table. No air-conditioning, no TV, no telephone. A lonely light bulb hung dispiritedly from the middle of the ceiling. The sheet on the mattress was clean, although there was no top sheet, no blanket. 'I'd like another sheet, though.'

He gave a crooked smile. 'You're supposed to wrap yourself in your sarong.'

'Sorry, it's at the cleaners.'

Nick spoke to the old man who was patiently waiting for them to decide. He gave Megan a curious look, then nodded. He probably thinks I'm weird, wanting another sheet, she thought, and gave him a smile, which he returned politely.

'OK, that's settled,' Nick said as the man disappeared down the gloomy passage. 'Let's get our luggage up here and then go out and find something to eat.'

They found dinner in a large *warung*, an outside restaurant with only a roof to keep it safe from the elements. The food was cooked in large woks placed over fires made in big oil drums, and the procedure could be watched while sitting at the tables.

'You're ready for something hot and spicy?' Nick asked.

'Sure. I'm hungry.' She played with the napkins that had been placed in a water glass in the middle of the table, discovering they had all been carefully cut in half for economy's sake.

Nick surveyed the menu. 'There's all kinds of meat—chicken, crab, frog's legs, cuttle-fish. Take your pick.'

'I'll leave it to you. I like everything.'

'Good. I can't tolerate picky eaters.'

A variety of dishes, hot from the fire, arrived at the table, and Megan tried them all, drinking cold beer to douse the fires. There was little conversation. We're both tired, she thought. I'm glad we won't have to drive all day tomorrow.

They would visit a housing development in the morning and have lunch with a couple of business people. After that, they would set off again and make a start on the next part of the trip.

They walked back to the hotel in the warm night air. Here and there, small food stalls stood by the road, illuminated by small kerosene lamps. People stood around, eating and talking.

'It's still early,' said Nick. 'Is there anything you'd like to do?'

'I'm tired. I think I'll just go to bed. Maybe I'll read for a while.'

He nodded. 'All right. I'll see you in the morning. Seven o'clock, all right?'

'Fine.'

Taking a shower was an experience. There was no shower in the little bathroom. A square, tiled tub, waist-high, was filled with clean, cold water. A blue plastic dipper with a long handle lay on the edge. The floor was tiled and had a drainage hole. Megan scooped up a pan of water, gritted her teeth and poured it over herself. After a good soaping, she repeated the procedure until her body was clean and soapless again, and she was shivering with cold.

Oh, well, this is supposed to build character, she told herself as she dried herself with the small, thin towel furnished by the hotel. At least you're clean. Cold, but clean. She shivered. I'd kill for a cup of hot tea, she thought.

She pulled on a cotton terrycloth robe and opened the door. The gloomy passage, with its single light bulb, did not invite exploration. Maybe there's no kitchen here, she thought. Well, of course there is—there has to be. She looked down at herself. The robe only reached half-way down her thighs. This was no way to go wandering through the place, not in this country, anyway. She grimaced. I'll have to get dressed again, she thought. Oh, hell, forget the tea! She closed the door, found her book and lay down on the mattress, pulling the extra sheet over her.

Ten minutes later there was a knock on her door. Megan

leaped out of bed and pulled on the robe. 'Who is it?'

'Nick.'

She unlocked the door. 'Something wrong?' Then she saw in his hands the small round metal tray with the two tall glasses with steaming tea, and her eyes flew up to his grinning face.

'Nothing's wrong. I thought I'd bring you your tea.'

She stood there, not knowing what to say. Nick didn't move, but just stood there, waiting patiently with the tray in his hands.

'Thank you,' she said at last, reaching out for one of the glasses, but it was too hot to touch and she jerked back her hand.

'Let me put it down for you.'

Megan didn't move. She didn't want him in her room.

He let out a sigh. 'For heaven's sake, woman, move! This stuff is hot!'

She stepped aside, holding on to the door. 'Just put it on the table.'

He set the tray down, then looked at her, one eyebrow raised in question. 'May I join you?'

'No. But thank you for the tea. I appreciate it.' She was still standing at the door, holding it open, her message clear.

He strolled over to her, stopping right in front of her and looking into her eyes. For a long moment he just stood there, looking at her, and she felt her nerves jangle with his closeness.

'I'm tired of your ice-maiden act,' he said slowly, dangerously. 'I'm tired of your hostility.' He took the doorhandle out of her grip and closed it. 'Stop acting like a neurotic. Sit down and drink your damned tea!'

CHAPTER FOUR

NICK gripped Megan's arm, propelled her over to the bed and make her sit down. His anger set off a shiver of fear, and for a moment she was too shocked to protest.

He towered over her. 'I was trying to be *nice* to you,' he hit out. 'I'm trying to find some sort of harmony, so we can make this trip less of an ordeal. The least I expect from you is to meet me half-way!'

She rubbed her tender arm; his grasp had been less than gentle. 'And meeting you half-way means sitting here having a cosy cup of tea and chatting amiably about the day's events? After which you'll tuck me in, say goodnight and leave? How gullible do you think I am?'

'Not as gullible as you used to be, obviously,' he said coldly.

'I don't know what it is you expect of me! What is it you're after? I spent all day with you! I have to sit next to you, look at you, talk to you, eat with you. Can't I have the evening to myself?' Her anger was overpowering her fear. 'There's no need for you to come to my room, carrying my evening tea! Or were you expecting an exchange of favours? Life the good old days? Well, you can forget it!'

His body tensed. Anger radiated from him. 'Are you afraid I might force myself on you?'

'After that scene in the bathroom in the Borobudur Hotel, I wouldn't put it past you!'

His face went rigid. 'Have I ever, *ever* forced myself on you in the past? Have my attentions *ever* been unwelcome?'

'They certainly were in the bathroom a couple of days ago!' snapped Megan furiously.

'Were they?'

'Yes!'

'Don't fool yourself, Megan. You may hate me. You may resent the fact that I'm your boss on the most important job you've ever had, but you know as well as I do that we are still very much attracted to each other.'

She laughed coldly. 'You must be dreaming!'

'I'm not dreaming, and you know it. You feel it like I feel it. It's always there when we're together. Your hostility is just a defensive barrier you're throwing up because you don't want to accept the truth.'

She tilted her head and gave him a derisive look. 'You're not bad, Dr Freud. Now, what is all this in aid of? Are you trying to pursuade me that maybe we should give in to our animal urges, and start off where we left off two years ago? Are you thinking that, as long as we're going to be ensconced on a small island for a while, we might as well make the best of it, have a convenient affair, no strings attached, a friendly goodbye when the project is finished?'

'No,' he said coldly, 'that's not what I was thinking.'

'Well, good! It would be too risky an undertaking for you, wouldn't it?'

Nick cocked one eyebrow. 'Oh?'

'I might just smother you again, suffocate you, cramp your style.'

He paled under his tan. 'That's hitting below the belt.'

'Oh, is it? Well, I'm so sorry!'

He let out a sigh. 'Megan, I know it's not easy for you to spend so much time with me,' he began slowly. 'I realise you haven't come to terms with . . .'

'Stop right there!' Anger rushed to her head in a wave of heat. 'I don't need any more of your analysing, all right? Maybe *you* should have your head examined!'

He closed his eyes wearily, his shoulders slumping fractionally. 'I don't believe this! I come here with the best of intentions, and here we are in the middle of a battle. All I did was bring you an innocent cup of tea for the simple reason that I remember you . . .'

'And I remember, too! And I'd prefer to for . . . forget.' To her horror, her voice shook and tears burned behind her eyes. She swallowed at the constriction in her throat.

Nick's eyes narrowed and she looked away. Why had she said that? It was stupid to let him know the memories still hurt. She wished they didn't. She wished she could just go on pretending there had been nothing between them, but it seemed to be impossible. With every turn there was something else that brought the past back. A gesture, a word, a stupid cup of tea.

Nick moved away from her, sat down on the only chair and leaned back wearily.

'Megan,' he said softly, 'you may not believe this, but I never meant to hurt you.'

'Well, you did,' she said coldly. 'I deserved better than for you to walk out on me the way you did.'

'I know. And I'm sorry.'

She forced back the old pain, felt herself grow cold and unfeeling again. She shrugged carelessly. 'Well, it hardly matters now. I was young and stupid, and it's a long time ago.'

His eyes met hers. 'But not long enough.'

She gave him a look of cold dislike. 'Don't flatter yourself!'

'I didn't mean to hurt you,' he repeated. 'It was the last thing I wanted, but it was unavoidable, Megan. I had to be honest with myself. I had to be honest with you. Feeling the way I did then, it would never have worked between us.'

'I don't want to talk about it.' She tried to sound cool and indifferent, but her hand was shaking as she reached for the tea. She withdrew it before picking up the glass, afraid she'd slosh the tea all over herself.

Nick picked up his glass of tea and took a swallow. 'I think it's cooled down enough to drink,' he said, dropping the subject like a brick.

Good. Megan drank some of her own tea. It tasted funny.

'I had a hell of a time rustling up somebody to fix it for me,' he went on conversationally. 'Finally found a sweet little thing of fourteen or so who obliged. She was just about to pour half a pound of sugar in the tea when I yelled at her not to. She looked scared to death. Must be my accent.' He took another gulp of tea and watched her drink hers.

'Do you like it?' he asked, apparently intent on getting some response from her.

Megan shrugged. 'It's different. I'll get used to it.' She was sitting on the edge of the bed, unable to relax. She just wanted to get this over with, get him out of her room.

'It's a local tea. If you ever order tea, tell them you want *teh pahit*, bitter tea, as opposed to sweet tea. If you don't, they'll automatically put ten spoons of sugar in it; that's the way they drink it here.'

'*Teh pahit,*' she repeated dutifully. 'I'll try and remember.' She hadn't expected a language lesson. Well, it didn't matter. Anything, anything.

She tried not to look at him, but her gaze kept returning to his face, his hands. And in her heart she wished for one crazy moment that they could move back in time. Wished that for just a short time she could experience again the loving they had shared, know again the joy of freely expressing her feelings for him, trusting he would not betray her.

She'd made herself so vulnerable, so terribly vulnerable.

But the past could not be brought back, and it was probably just as well. She wouldn't want, ever again, to have to go through the heartbreak that had followed that blissful time of innocence.

'I tried to figure out what they serve for breakfast,' Nick said after a silence. 'It looks like fried rice, or bread and margarine.'

'That's fine.' She had no small talk in her. She finished the tea as fast as she could, almost choking on it, and put the glass back on the round metal tray. Doing the same, he came to his feet. 'I should be going. I'll see you at seven in the morning.' He opened the door, wished her goodnight and closed it firmly behind him.

Megan looked at the two empty tea glasses on the table, feeling a sudden violent misery rise inside her. She closed her eyes tightly and clenched her hands into fists, trying to suppress the wild urge to take the glasses and smash them on the floor.

In the days that followed, they travelled many miles, past endless rice paddies where women worked, bent over, wearing conical hats against the sun; through rubber forests and past fields of sugar cane; through small villages where children waved and chickens and goats ran across the road; through larger towns full of noise and colour and the spicy smells of cooking food—open-air markets and traffic and food stalls and mosques.

Megan took many pictures—of fishing-boats, of ancient temples, of children playing with sticks and cans, of bullock carts and brightly painted bicycle-cabs, of women at work, making pots.

Sometimes she would ask Nick to stop, which he usually did without complaint, sometimes not. When he was in a hurry he got irritated with her, but she ignored it and did what she wanted to do. A good picture was worth a little inconvenience.

'I didn't know you were such a photographer,' he commented one day after she'd spent ten minutes getting just one shot.

'I wasn't. It's a new passion.' Putting the lens cap on, she hopped back into the car. 'Thanks for stopping.'

'Sure.' He started the engine, waiting for a truck loaded high with rattan baskets full of chickens to pass them, then pulled out on to the road. 'When did you take up photography?'

'Couple of years ago. Before I went to Chad.' She took a

banana from the back seat and began to peel it. 'I took a lot of horrible pictures of the desert. Very difficult to do.'

He gave a crooked smile. 'Too much sand.'

'Right,' she agreed, her mouth full of banana. They were having one of those polite little conversations again, with Nick trying to draw her out. Megan didn't want to be drawn out. She took another bite of banana.

She'd taken up photography soon after Nick had left her. She'd bought herself a good camera, taken several courses, read through a stack of books and become quite an accomplished amateur. In the end, she'd even managed to get some passable pictures of the desert, although nothing that could be submitted to the *National Geographic*.

'I bet you're good,' he said. 'You're the creative type.'

'I suppose I enjoy it because it's creative. It's interesting to compose a picture, to look through the viewfinder, get the right angle, the right lighting, get the right composition of shape and colour, of light and shadow.'

'You sound good, too,' said Nick, grinning.

'Yeah.' She tossed the banana peel out of the window, into the bamboo growing by the road. 'Biodegradable,' she explained in answer to Nick's frown. 'Great fertiliser for bamboo, didn't you know?'

'Bamboo needs fertiliser like I need a hole in the head!'

'All right, if you want to go back, I'm more than willing to fish it out of the bamboo, if I can still find it.'

'I wouldn't want to go to that extreme.'

Megan grinned. 'I didn't think so.' She stretched and yawned. 'I hope this place we're sleeping in tonight has better mattresses. My back is killing me!'

Every night they stayed in different places—tiny rented rooms at a *losmen*, with nothing but a bed and a chair, or in hotels of varying degrees of comfort. Before falling asleep she would listen to the noises coming from outside—the metallic tunes of *gamelan* music, or some solitary flautist celebrating the night. In the morning, the cooing of doves and the twittering of a variety of birds made for a gentle awakening.

Megan enjoyed the early mornings and the evenings, when there was a reprieve from the tension that marked her relationship with Nick. The long hours on the road with him were shredding her nerves.

They drove for hours on end, visited housing developments, holding meetings, all with a veneer of politeness. For long stretches they would go without speaking to each other. She'd look out of the window, enjoying the scenery, or sometimes just sleep, with her head on a folded towel.

'You're very quiet,' he said, on the third day, after an endless silence.

'I've nothing to say.'

'In that case, it's better not to say it.'

'You're right,' Megan agreed.

'Especially when you don't want to talk anyway.'

'Right again.'

'You didn't used to be so quiet. I never knew you not wanting to talk. Remember that night we sat up till . . .'

'No.'

'Sure you do. It was the day we . . .'

'Oh, just shut up and drive!' Megan turned her face away and closed her eyes. He was always reminding her of the past, of things they had said or done. It irritated her no end. The last thing she wanted was to think of the past.

She pictured an exotic garden, birds, flowers. A place to be alone, to be quiet. No Nick. No blue eyes looking at her all the time, no undercurrents, no tensions. Just peace.

Sometimes she was caught off guard and found they had lapsed into an old, familiar friendliness, but somehow it never lasted. There was always something to ruin the comfort of the relaxed atmosphere between them. Underneath it all there were too many tensions, too many vibrations.

Nick had been right.

'Don't just sit there, do something!'

Nick's dark eyebrows rose in question. 'What would you have me do?'

Megan looked at the endless line of cars ahead, all stopped, all baking in the midday heat. 'Fly!'

His mouth quirked. 'Unfortunately, this car didn't come equipped with wings.'

'You're a lousy James Bond!'

'I'm afraid you're right.'

For half an hour, thirty endless minutes, they had been standing still, waiting for the removal of some unknown obstruction somewhere up ahead. Megan was hot and thirsty. She was also dusty and sticky, and she was losing her temper. Not at Nick this time, which was an improvement. Thank God, the trip was nearly over. Tomorrow they would take the ferry and be on Bali. Then she would have her own house, a place to get away from Nick for at least part of the day, a place to eat her meals by herself.

In the job situation she would still have to manage.

Once, she'd dreamed of this—a job assignment with Nick, travelling together to some alien place, learning about other people, their pain and pleasures. Being together all the time. So, here we are, she thought derisively, a dream come true. Bali, here we come!

If ever they'd get moving again . . . She peered down the road. Nothing but cars. Chrome and glass glittered in the sun. Above the hot tarmac road, air shimmered like water.

'There's no traffic on the other lane. Nothing's coming this way.' As she spoke, a car passed them, having broken out of line, and careened down the wrong side of the road. A moment later, another one followed.

'All right, let's try it,' Nick said, moving the car into the other lane. 'We'll probably end up in one hell of a mess up ahead, but anything is better than just sitting here feeling like a failed hero.'

The mess was closer than expected. A little ahead of them, the owner of a brand new shiny Mercedes was losing patience too. He moved out of line without looking back and ran right into the side of their van. A scraping of metal, an explosive curse from Nick as he slammed on the brakes and both cars were stopped. Megan's heart jumped in her throat, then settled back when she realised that nothing terribly serious had happened—no bloody bodies, no screaming wounded.

They jumped out to assess the damage—a minor scrape down the length of the van. Megan's immediate reaction was relief, which was not shared by the owner of the Mercedes, who had come up to them with fury glittering in his eyes. He was impeccably dressed in dark trousers and a long-sleeved batik dress-shirt, and was probably on his way to some important meeting or appointment.

'You were on the wrong side of the road!' he exclaimed in English.

Nick's eyebrows rose in amused surprise. 'The same place you were going, sir.'

The Mercedes had suffered greater damage: a headlight smashed, a door dented and scraped. It was a sorry sight on such an luxurious car.

'I want the police!' the man announced, ignoring Nick's logic. 'When we get moving again, I'll meet you at the next police station!' He began to write down the Mitsubishi's licence number.

'You should have looked back to check the traffic before moving into the other lane, sir,' Nick said calmly. 'It wasn't my fault, it was yours. Simple negligence.'

The man did not answer, and strode back to his car to mourn the damage some more.

'He must know he's at fault,' Megan said. 'Why does he want to go to the police?'

'Because we're foreigners. With a little help from the police, he's going to make us pay up.'

'Great!' An idea hit her and she took her camera from the car. Ignoring the man's furious stare, she walked around the scene of the accident and took pictures, worrying not about artistic quality this time, but clarity of record. As she did so, she noticed that for some incomprehensible reason the Mercedes did not have a rear-view mirror. She snapped a shot of that, too, stepping out of the way only just in time, as the man started the engine and drove off down the wrong side of the road.

'I'll see you at the police station!' he called through the window.

Megan climbed back in her seat and found Nick behind the wheel, grinning at her. He tapped the camera in her lap. 'Now that was a brilliant idea,' he said.

She smiled smugly. 'I thought so, too.'

'Quick thinking. My compliments, madam.'

'Thank you.' She felt a glow of satisfaction.

He put the car in gear, just as the line began to move slowly. They inched their way back into the line.

They never did find out what had caused the delay. At the police station in the next town, no shiny blue Mercedes was waiting for them.

'My camera saved the day,' Megan said.

'No, you did.' Nick's eyes smiled warmly into hers, and for a moment she felt a lightness, a happiness she hadn't felt for a long time.

Bali was as gorgeous as Megan remembered: lush green countryside, rice paddies, hills. Idyllic sounds—the babble of small streams, the twittering of exotic birds, the laughter of dark-eyed children. Bright colours—the sarongs, the altar offerings by the road, hibiscus, frangipani.

The town of Denpasar teemed with life. The streets were

crowded with a variety of vehicles—minibuses, horse-drawn carts, *bemos*, motor-cycles and movable food stalls. People were everywhere—women carrying loads on their heads, tourists in shorts, schoolchildren in uniforms, pedlars selling ice, balloons, wood carvings.

It had been a long day's drive by the time they arrived at the hotel, and after a quick dinner Megan went up to her room and went to bed. She slept soundly through the night. Going down for breakfast the next morning, she found a note from Nick saying she could take it easy for the rest of the morning and he would see her at lunch.

Megan frowned, not knowing what was going on, then shrugged and ate her breakfast. She spent the morning wandering through Denpasar, taking in the colourful hustle and bustle in the streets, and browsing through little shops. Tomorrow, they would leave for the village of Ubud, not far from the capital, and see about their houses and office. She was eager to get started.

As she got ready for lunchj, the red light on her phone signalled a message.

'It's from Mr Donovan,' said the desk clerk. 'He cannot meet you for lunch, but he'll see you later this afternoon.'

If she'd known where he'd gone, it wouldn't have irritated her so. What was he up to? What was she supposed to do all day? Hang around?

There were worse things than hanging around in a nice hotel without Nick in attendance. A nice change, actually. Megan had a sumptuous lunch—a huge shrimp salad, fresh baked croissants and rich, dark coffee. After all that, she got so sleepy, she had a lazy nap, followed by tea and cake on the terrace, where Nick found her later that afternoon.

'Hello there, beautiful!' He sat down at her table.

'Where have you been all day?'

He looked at her derisively. 'You sound like an annoyed wife! I thought you'd be happy to have the day to yourself.'

Annoyed wife! It irked her more than she was willing to admit. 'I would have appreciated knowing where you were.'

He grinned. 'You felt deserted?'

'Oh, for God's sake!'

'Hey, calm down! Is there more tea?' He looked into the pot. A saronged waitress came gliding over, a creamy white frangipani blossom in her hair, a serene smile on her beautiful face.

'More tea, sir?' A soft, melodious voice.

'Please.'

'Would you like a piece of cake?'

'No, thank you.' He rubbed his stomach and gave the girl a cheerful smile. 'I'm full of Balinese duck.' She giggled delightedly, picked up the teapot with one small, delicate hand and moved away with a fluid swing of her hips. Nick stretched out, expelling a deep sigh, and glanced around with lazy contentment. Then he looked back at Megan.

'Oh, yes! About my escapades today—first I went to the airport to see about our airfreight. It was all there and I checked it out. It's in the van. Then I went to the Ministry and told them we've arrived, and I checked up on the housing.'

'And that took all day?'

'Just about. You know how it goes,' he said with maddening calm. 'The man you want to see isn't there, but is coming back later. Then they want you to meet some of the other people, introduce you around. You talk. Then Number One man arrives. You talk some more. Then they take you out to lunch.'

She nodded. 'Balinese duck?'

'Right. Then they told me all their problems.'

'What problems?' Megan didn't like the sound of that. She didn't trust his casual tone.

'About your house. There's a snag, I'm afraid.'

'Great. Just what I need. What is it?'

'You can't move into your house yet. The guy in it extended for a month because of some emergency with his project.'

'I thought they told us everything was arranged already!' she protested.

'It was—supposedly. But the Ministry of Agriculture, who are renting it now, kindly requested the Ministry of Housing to let them have it for their man for an extra month. And of course, they agreed, hoping that we could see their point. It didn't make much sense to me to start off on a bad foot, so for the sake of friendly co-operation I let them off the hook.'

'You did? Well, how generous of you! And what am I supposed to do in the meantime?'

'Move in with me.'

She stared at him, furious. 'You've got to be kidding!'

He shrugged. 'I don't see why it's a problem. It seems my house is big enough to accommodate us both for a month.'

No house was big enough for that! 'Why doesn't the man move into a hotel and let me have my house?'

'He has a family. Three little kids, including a small baby. It didn't seem fair.'

She had to admit he had a point. 'Well, then, I'll stay at the Horizon.'

'For a month? I'm afraid we don't have that in the budget.'

'I'll find something else! One of those little *losmens* . . .' She was beginning to lose her cool. He was taking this far too casually, and it made her mad.

'Don't be childish, Megan. My house is big enough. Surely we can manage for one month?'

She took a deep breath, the frustrations and tensions suddenly overwhelming her. 'There's a curse on this job, you know that? You know what I thought when I first read the project description? *It's too good to be true.* And it sure is! First I heard you're the one who designed it. Next I'm told you'll be the project director. Then we're supposed to careen all over Java together, and now *this*! And I haven't even started the damned job yet! I wonder what's next!'

'I suppose, with a bit of creativity, we could come up with a number of scenarios.'

She didn't miss the gleam in his eyes. 'I don't even want to think about it!'

'Why not? It might be interesting.' His tone held amusement. 'Lighten up, Meggie. We're on Bali. We're supposed to have fun.'

She glared at him. 'Don't *Meggie* me!' She shoved her chair back, just as the waitress came floating back to their table with a fresh pot of tea and a clean cup.

'Don't leave,' Nick said. 'Join me for a cup.'

'No, thanks. I've had enough.'

'Tea or me?'

'Both!'

Nick have the waitress a helpless look. 'The lady is angry,' he said regretfully. 'She's always angry with me.'

The girl gave Megan a wide-eyed glance, then looked back at Nick, at a loss for words.

'Can you believe it?' he asked conversationally. 'I'm such a nice guy, and she doesn't like me.'

'He's full of it,' Megan said, and the girl looked at her, uncomprehending.

'I don't think she got that,' Nick said.

'He's a liar,' Megan corrected, smiling at the girl. 'He's not nice at all. Does he *look* nice?'

The girl nodded, her dark eyes suddenly shining with laughter. 'He looks . . . handsome. And—eh—very *strong*. It's better not be angry with him.' She tossed Nick a teasing smile and swayed away gracefully.

'Hah!' Nick said triumphantly. 'She told you!'

Megan bit her lip to suppress a smile.

'Well?' he asked expectantly.

'Well, what?'

'Well, was she right, our little dark-eyed beauty?'

'Right about what?'

He leaned closer towards her, the familiar, irresistible smile creeping into his eyes. 'You know about what.'

'No, I don't.'

'You're trying not to laugh.' His eyes taunted her.

'No, I'm not!' Megan bit her lip and looked away, but the smile forced its way out.

'It's better not be angry with me,' he whispered across the table. 'Hah, you're smiling! Now tell me, was she right?'

She let the smile go free. 'I guess she was.'

He leaned back in his chair and nodded smugly. 'It takes a wise woman to admit her mistake.'

'Don't push it.'

He grinned and picked up the teapot. 'Now, have another cuppa. I'll be mum.'

'You what?'

'I'll be mum. It's an English expression, it means I'll pour the tea.'

Megan moved the chair closer to the table and held out her cup. 'Please.'

For a moment, his intense blue eyes held hers, the laughter still there. 'Let's make the best of it, shall we?' he asked, his voice light, yet with an undertone of gravity.

Megan nodded. 'All right.'

She wished he wouldn't look at her like that.

The flower was perfect. A crimson, bell-shaped hibiscus—a delicate perfection of brilliant red, velvety petals and long, slender stamens.

Megan smiled at Nick, taking the flower from him. He looked devastatingly attractive in his batik shirt and dark trousers, blue eyes bright and intent on her face, oozing male charm.

'Thank you, it's beautiful.' She could not help but be surprised. It was totally out of character for him to offer her this flower. He'd never once brought her flowers before.

'I stole it from the garden. Tuck it behind your ear, and then let's go down and have some dinner.'

She did as he requested, feeling suddenly deliciously frivolous. A touch of Bali, she decided as she examined herself in the dresser mirror. The red flower looked rather exotic against her dark hair. A nice splash of colour as well, in contrast to the white of her dress. Just as well I wasn't wearing purple, she thought to herself.

'An island maiden,' commented Nick, smiling at her reflection. She wished, for a fleeting moment, that she could see into his head, read his thoughts. Why had he given her this crimson bloom, when he'd never before made such a gesture? She shook the feeling away, catching Nick's gaze as he watched her face in the mirror.

'What were you thinking just now?' he asked.

'Oh, never mind.'

'I'd like to know,' he said softly, his blue eyes charming her into an answer.

Had her expression given her away? 'I was wondering why you gave me a flower. It seems such a . . . romantic gesture for a man like you.'

'Bali is a romantic island,' he said, the tempting smile still lurking in the blue depths of his eyes. 'And you're the beautiful woman I'm taking out to dinner on our first night here.'

Megan nodded. 'That seems like a good reason,' she returned lightly. Picking up her clutch bag and key, she turned away from the mirror.

Nick's hand rested lightly on her shoulder as he guided her to the door. It was the first time he had touched her in days. It was nothing but a casual gesture, yet she was intently aware of the warmth of his hand on her shoulder.

She wished he wouldn't touch her.

He reached out to open the door and his eyes caught hers, and for a moment his hand stopped in mid-air. Then, slowly, his eyes still holding hers, both hands came up and took her face between them.

Megan couldn't move; she was mesmerised by his eyes, a deep intense blue, and his mouth, firm and inviting. Her heart began to beat in frantic rhythm, and every nerve tingled with anticipation. He was going to kiss her, and for this one thrilling, heart-stopping moment she wanted him to. His face moved closer and his features blurred. Then there was the warmth of his mouth as it covered hers, a warmth that spread all through her. It was a gentle yet sensuous kiss that made her blood sing, but didn't last nearly long enough.

He backed away almost immediately, smiling crookedly. 'I couldn't resist,' he whispered. Then, abruptly, he opened the door and followed her out.

Once in the corridor he was suddenly all business again. 'Where do you want to eat?' he asked. 'Here, in the hotel, or would you prefer somewhere else?'

She averted her gaze, afraid he'd see the disappointment in her eyes, hating herself for feeling the way she did. 'I don't want to climb back in that car if I have a choice. Here's fine.' It took an effort to make her voice sound calm. 'I couldn't resist', he'd said. Obviously I can't either, she thought in despair. One simple kiss and I'm all off balance.

Nick pushed the elevator button. 'Out on the terrace or inside?'

'On the terrace. I love eating outside,' she said, covering up her shakiness with a flow of words. 'It's what I like about Europe, you know—all those little sidewalk cafés where you can watch the world go by. And those quiet country inns where you sit outside and enjoy the scenery while you eat.'

He gave a half-smile. 'You're a romantic—you always were. Candles all over the house, schmaltzy music. You forced crocuses and hyacinths in the kitchen window because you couldn't wait for spring.'

The elevator doors opened and she stepped aside to let a tall, thin Chinese pass, distracting her from a painful jolt of

memory. It seemed strange to hear Nick talk about this; the
memories always seemed to be just hers—private, unshared.
But they were his, too, and to hear him mention them now
made it seem as if he were intruding in her mind, exposing
what lay hidden there.

They stepped aside. Nick pushed the button and the door
glided closed. They were silent as the elevator swiftly
descended to the ground floor. Megan glanced over at the
tall, dark man next to her, wondering what it was he felt
when he remembered the girl she'd been two years ago, and
the candles and the crocuses on the window-sill.

CHAPTER FIVE

'YOU'VE no idea how much I appreciate this,' Kathy Ingram said, as she smiled at Megan and patted the baby's back. A burp was being awaited, but apparently was not forthcoming. 'Come on, love, let's have it now,' Kathy implored.

'It's no problem, really,' said Megan. 'Nick's house is big enough.' How convincing I sound, she thought to herself as she looked around the cheeful room. But Kathy Ingram was so genuinely grateful to be able to stay in the house for another month, Megan didn't have the heart to tell her how very much she would have like to be in the house herself, to be away from Nick and the tension that seemed to build insidiously under the surface, despite all her efforts to keep her emotions under control. They were making the best of it, getting along carefully, but still her nerves were on edge, just being close to him.

And she knew what it was. It was not her dislike of him, her anger, or the pain of what had happened long ago. It was what it had always been—that primitive, basic emotion between them. It was still there and it always would be. She didn't know how to combat it.

Five days ago, they had arrived in the village, settled in the house as best they could, and started work at the district office of the Ministry—interviewing and hiring a secretary, and a driver-cum-office messenger. Their office was a drab, grey room that needed cheering rather badly. Megan had been tempted to bring in a bowl of the orange, pink and white bougainvillaea that grew rampantly in Nick's garden, but decided against it. It wasn't only her office. She didn't

want to tempt Nick into commenting on her love for flowers.
Her love for candles, schmaltzy music. He seemed to find
some perverse enjoyment in reminding her of the past.

'Let me show you the house,' Kathy said, 'and then we'll
have some tea. The kitchen isn't great, by our standards,' she
apologised as she showed Megan the small, dark room with
nothing more than the very basic sink, counter space, stove
and refrigerator, 'but, to tell you the truth, I don't spend much
time there. I prepare the baby's food, but Ariaso, our cook,
takes care of all the meals for the rest of the family.'

'I'm no cook,' Megan assured her. 'I'll be more than glad to
leave it to someone else.'

'Ariaso is available, if you like. She's looking for a job, now
that we're leaving. We like her, but you can see for yourself.
She's very independent. She does all the market shopping for
meat and fish, vegetables and fruit, and her cooking is
wonderful. I drive into Denpasar once a week or so, and go to
the supermarket for jam and coffee and milkpowder and that
sort of thing.'

They moved on to the rest of the house. Megan had liked
the house on sight. It was a low, brick bungalow with a red-
tiled roof, shaded by tall coconut palms and surrounded by a
lush tropical garden. There was a living-room, a dining-room,
a small bathroom and three bedrooms.

'It beats my apartment in DC hands down,' Megan said. 'I
love all this space.

'It's not luxurious, by any means, and it could use a coat of
paint, but I've enjoyed living here.' Kathy looked wistful. 'I
like Bali. It's beautiful and peaceful, and we've made such
good friends here. I don't know if I can adjust to Sydney again.
The life is so hectic there, and I'm not looking forward to
dealing with three little ones without servants.' She grimaced.
'Don't let them hear me at home!'

They had tea on the veranda that overlooked the garden.
Banana bushes flourished in one corner, and several pawpaw

trees promised an abundance of fruit. Other houses were not far, but they were hidden by greenery. Nick's house was only a short walk away.

It was Saturday afternoon, and Nick had gone into Denpasar in search of some tools and electrical equipment he needed. Megan had decided to explore the area, find the house and introduce herself.

Kathy had been delighted to see her. She was alone with the baby; the older children were playing at the house of a friend. Her husband was at his worksite, working all weekend to get the job finished in the little time still available, and he wouldn't be home until late at night. She invited Megan to stay for dinner and Megan accepted, pleased.

It was almost nine when Megan finally made it back to Nick's house, finding everything in darkness and no Nick. She switched on the lights and wandered aimlessly through the empty rooms, wondering what could possibly have detained him in Denpasar. 'I'll be back by six or so,' he'd said. That was more than three hours ago. It had been dark for that long, and driving in the dark was not advisable—cars without lights, people in dark clothes on the road, bikes without reflectors, buses passing around blind corners.

Maybe he had met people in town and had dinner with them. Maybe the car had broken down. Maybe he'd been in an accident. Maybe he was hurt! Dead!

There you go again, Megan thought derisively. If he knew what you're thinking, he'd say you sound like a worried wife.

Well, she wasn't a wife and she wasn't worried. Nick Donovan could take care of himself. There would be a good reason he hadn't come back yet. He was probably at the bar at the Horizon, entertaining some swishy lady. Not really his style, though, she had to admit.

She got ready for bed, made herself some tea and tried to read. It didn't work. It was now almost ten, and still no Nick. No phone call, no message of any sort. Damn him!

I'm not worried, she told herself, as she went into the kitchen to find something to eat. She shouldn't be hungry after all the food Kathy had fed her, or rather, Kathy's cook, Ariaso, a minuscule Balinese woman of indeterminate age with a friendly smile and laughing brown eyes.

There was a round blue tin of Danish butter cookies she'd bought in a little shop in the village. She got back into bed, can in her lap, and tried to read again while she munched the cookies.

She'd managed to consume half the can when she heard a car come up the drive. It didn't sound like the Mitsubishi. Megan put on her robe, ran to the front door and looked out the side window.

The car was a taxi, and a man was limping towards the house. A man with his arm in a white sling that shone in the dark. She tore open the door.

'Nick!' she exclaimed.

'Where the hell were you?' he ground out as he limped past her into the house. Once in the light, his face shocked her. He looked deathly pale, and a dark bruise decorated his forehead. His arm was bandaged and his trousers were torn at the knee. Fear rushed through her and she stared at him in alarm.

'What happened?'

'Where were you?' he repeated, eyes furious.

'Where was I?' The tone of his voice enraged her, momentarily overwhelming her concern. He was very obviously not on the brink of death, although he certainly didn't look far from it. 'What do you mean, where was I? What about you? It's eleven o'clock at night! I've been thinking . . . oh, forget it!' She closed the door behind him.

Nick faced her, eyes grim. 'I've been trying to call you all damn afternoon and evening! Where the hell were you?'

She clenched her hands into fists, trying to control her temper. 'I wasn't aware I was under house arrest! I went over to meet Kathy Ingram. I had tea with her, then she asked me to stay for dinner. I didn't get back until after nine.'

He moved slowly over to a chair and lowered himself in it, wincing with pain.

Megan stood in front of him. 'Will you please tell me what happened?'

'I fell into an open drainage hole in the street.'

'Oh, no!' she exclaimed in a low voice.

He grimaced. 'I was lucky. It was dry.'

'How did you fall in? Didn't you see it?'

'Of course I saw it! I was crossing the street. A motor-cycle with mama, papa, son and baby daughter all cosily clumped together, ran a red light. I jumped aside and *whammo*! tripped on the cement edge of the kerb and fell in the hole. Broke my arm, bruised my ribs, bust my head and knee, but otherwise I'm fine, thank you.'

'You broke your arm? Why don't you have a cast?'

'I'll get one on Monday. It's a simple break and they want the swelling to go down first.'

'What about the people on the motor-cycle?'

'They went on their merry way. They might not even have noticed.'

'Oh, Nick, I'm sorry. You must feel terrible.'

'Not as bad as I did hanging in that hole,' he assured her drily.

'Did anybody help you?'

'Every man, woman and child in the street. I was quite an attraction, believe me! Somebody drove me to the hospital in his car. They took X-rays, doped me up, set my arm, tucked me into bed and told me to be a good boy and go to sleep.'

'So why didn't you?'

'For one thing, I was beginning to wonder about you. I'd been calling you and you weren't home. I wanted you to take a taxi, bail me out of the hospital and drive me back here. I kept calling and didn't get an answer. I was getting worried.'

Megan looked at him, incredulous. 'You can't be serious.

What could possibly happen to me in this place?'

For a moment, humour glinted in Nick's eyes. 'You could fall in a drainage hole, break your arm, bruise your ribs, bust your head and knee.'

'Then somebody would have taken me to the clinic. They'd have taken X-rays, doped me up, set my arm, tucked me into bed and told me to be a good girl and go to sleep.'

'And you would have, of course.'

'Not until they'd brought me a cup of *teh pahit*!'

'Of course.' Laughter flared briefly in his eyes, then he winced. He came to his feet and limped to the door. 'I'd better get to bed.'

'How did you get out of the hospital? Did you just walk out?'

'Yes.'

'Not too smart, if you ask me.'

'I didn't ask you, did I?' Nick's tone was mild. He was standing close to her now, leaning against the door jamb, looking at her with faint amusement. 'There's something . . .' He reached out his left hand and his thumb quickly brushed the corner of her mouth. 'A crumb. Have you been eating?'

'Cookies.'

'I thought you were in bed.'

'I was. I was eating them in bed, waiting for you. I ended up eating half the can and gaining three pounds in the process. All your fault.'

His mouth curled and his eyes began to gleam with the old familiar smile. 'You were waiting for me? If I'd known . . .'

She gave him a withering look. 'I was wondering what had happened to you.'

He held her gaze. 'All this mutual concern we have for each other is heart-warming, don't you think?'

'What I think is that you should go to sleep. You need anything? Aspirin?'

'Maybe later. But I do need ice to put around my arm, and

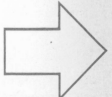

NO COST! NO OBLIGATION TO BUY! NO PURCHASE NECESSARY!

PLAY "LUCKY 7"
AND GET AS MANY AS SIX FREE GIFTS...

HOW TO PLAY:

1. With a coin, carefully scratch off the silver box at the right. This makes you eligible to receive one or more free books, and possibly other gifts, depending on what is revealed beneath the scatch-off area.

2. You'll receive brand-new Presents® novels. When you return this card, we'll send you the books and gifts you qualify for absolutely free!

3. Unless you tell us otherwise, every month we'll send you 8 additional novels to read and enjoy. If you decide to keep them, you'll pay only $1.99 per book*, a savings of 26¢ per book. There is no extra charge for postage and handling. There are no hidden extras.

4. When you join Harlequin Reader Service, we'll send you additional free gifts from time to time, as well as our newsletter.

5. You must be completely satisfied. You may cancel at any time just by dropping us a line or returning a shipment of books at our cost.

* Terms and prices subject to change.

DETACH AND MAIL CARD TODAY

BUSINESS REPLY CARD

First Class   Permit No. 717   Buffalo, NY

Postage will be paid by addressee

Harlequin Reader Service®
901 Fuhrmann Blvd.,
P.O. Box 1867
Buffalo, NY 14240-9952

NO POSTAGE
NECESSARY
IF MAILED
IN THE
UNITED STATES

I'll need help taking off my shirt.'

'How did you get it on?'

'Don't look so suspicious! One of the nurses had already cut off the sleeve at my request. It's possible to get it on, but I don't think the reverse is so easy.'

Megan followed him into his room. It was sparsely furnished, like her own, with a bed, a wardrobe and a chest of drawers. The curtainless windows were open and silver moonlight made a patch on Nick's bed. She heard the soothing babble of the rocky creek that ran through the back of the garden, and the whispering of the palms touched by the breeze.

Switching on the light, he sat down on the edge of the bed, and she watched him while he unbuttoned his shirt with his left hand. His blue eyes caught her gaze. 'Exciting, isn't it?' he said softly, taunting her.

She made a face at him. 'You hardly look like a Romeo tonight!'

Nick grinned. 'Don't look like a frightened virgin, then.'

'Don't say stupid things.'

His hand had reached the last button. The shirt fell open, revealing his bronzed chest with its mat of dark curly hair. She swallowed hard.

'Don't stand there, do something,' he encouraged. 'You're safe. With a bruised rib and a broken arm I'm quite harmless, believe me.'

'You've got one good arm,' she reminded him drily.

He lifted up his left arm and examined it. 'You're right. Not so harmless, after all. Was that an invitation?'

'No!'

He grinned. 'Are you going to take off my shirt, or are you just going to stand there and stare at my bare torso?'

Gritting her teeth, Megan reached out and slid the shirt off his good arm, then eased it over the injured one. As it came away, she felt an arm around her shoulders, pulling her aside, and she lost her balance and landed next to him on the side of the bed.

'Thank you,' he said, his face very close to hers.

'You're right, this arm works pretty well.'

'Let me go, Nick.'

'Why? Scared?'

'Why would I be scared?' It took an effort to sound casual. She wasn't feeling casual.

'Why, indeed?' His eyes probed hers.

Megan's heart began to beat frantically. She didn't like what was happening to her. She didn't like it that he could affect her so with merely a look, a word, a gesture. He was too close, his mouth only inches away.

She swallowed hard. 'Please, don't do this, Nick.'

'What am I doing?'

'You know what you're doing.' She felt warmth come into her cheeks. 'You know damn well what you're doing!'

His mouth silenced her, his lips closing over hers in a soft, sensuous contact. It caused a shockwave of emotion and she went limp with its force. It was a gentle, careful kiss, not at all what she had expected, and somehow she couldn't tear herself away. Her body leaped to life. She closed her eyes and her heart thumped with loud and laboured beats. She found herself responding to the gentleness, surrendering to the overwhelming sensation of sweet, sensuous longing that warmed and excited her all through. It was like a trance, a euphoria, a singing of the senses, caused by only this tender touch of lips and tongue.

When he released her she sat still for a long moment, afraid to breathe, afraid to look at him. She knew she should be angry with him for doing this, for bringing back all the old, familiar feelings, but there was no anger in her. How could she hate him for the slow, lingering lovingness of that kiss? He had loved her once; maybe this kiss was a remnant of the past, a memory brought back in touch.

She slowly got up and moved to the door without looking at him—she didn't have the courage for that.

'I'll get the ice for your arm.'

'Thank you.'

When she came back, Nick was in bed, the sheet pulled up to his waist. He looked pale and exhausted.

She'd put the ice-cubes in a plastic bag and wrapped it in a thin towel. She arranged it around his arm the way he told her.

'Does it hurt very much?' she asked.

'Some. I think the pain-killer they gave me is wearing off. I'd better have some aspirin.'

Ten minutes later Megan got back into bed, clearing it first of cookie crumbs. She was tired, yet couldn't sleep. She wished he hadn't kissed her. She wished she wasn't affected by him the way she was. Maybe it would always be that way. Maybe, once you loved someone the way she had loved Nick, you never got over it completely. Maybe the senses were imprinted so completely with that love that they would never forget and always respond.

Never forget . . . never forget . . . She didn't know why the words kept echoing in her head. She didn't know why, suddenly, tears were running down her cheeks.

She wished she'd never come to Bali.

Noises awoke her in the middle of the night. Something had fallen to the floor. What? Eyes and ears open, Megan listened. Somebody was moving around in the kitchen; it had to be Nick. She swung her feet over the edge of the bed, found her robe and put it on before investigating what was going on.

She found him in the kitchen, naked but for a pair of brief blue and white striped shorts. It wasn't an unfamiliar sight, but it had been a while since she had seen him dressed like this. Ice-cubes lay scattered all over the floor, and he was in the process of retrieving them.

'What's going on? What are you doing up in the middle of

the night?'

'I'm picking up ice-cubes!' Fury was barely restrained in his voice. 'The ice has melted. I was getting some more. I was trying to shake them loose with my left hand and, *voilà*, all over the damned floor!'

She bent down next to him and began picking up the cubes. 'Why didn't you call me?'

He gave her a sardonic look. 'And you would have come, Mommie?'

'You don't have to be sarcastic! Of course I would have come! You broke your arm, for God's sake! And I happen to be living in this house. You might as well thank the gods and take advantage of it.'

The corner of his mouth pulled down and his eyes sparked with a brief glimmer of humour.

'You know what I mean!' she added.

'Of course I do,' said Nick levelly. 'And you're right. I should have called. But I didn't. False pride, I suppose. Pigheadedness. Anything you'd like to call it.'

'Stupidity,' she offered.

'You don't need to go to extremes.' He sat down on a chair and groaned. 'Damn!'

Megan gave him a sharp look. 'Go back to bed. I'll bring you the ice. And if you need anything else, call me!'

'God, I love it when you act tough,' he muttered, coming to his feet and limping out the door.

She refilled the trays, put them back in the freezer and make the ice-pack. Nick was in bed, eyes closed, when she came in a few minutes later. She arranged the pack around his arm and he opened his eyes and looked at her.

'That's a prim and proper outfit you're wearing.'

'I'm a prim and proper woman.'

He gave a low, amused laugh. 'Hah! Since when?'

'Shut up and go to sleep.'

'I doubt that I will. Why don't you keep me company?'

'My tender ministrations don't go that far. I want to get some sleep.' She straightened away from him.

'You can sleep here. It's a big bed and I'm harmless ... well, almost.' He looked meaningfully at his left arm.

Megan did not bother replying, but walked to the door. 'Goodnight.'

'Spoil-sport!' he called after her.

She slept deeply for only a couple of hours, and woke to the twittering of the birds outside. It wasn't quite light yet and she hurried into a pair of white shorts and a red T-shirt, made some coffee and sat down on the veranda, watching dawn break over paradise. There was nothing more peaceful and idyllic than an early Balinese morning, with the birds greeting the sun with ecstatic chirping as the first tentative rays greened the palm leaves and transformed the flowering bushes into a blaze of colour.

'You're up early.' Nick stepped on to the veranda and sat down in a creaky rattan chair next to her, wincing with pain as he held his injured arm. He wore a pair of white running shorts, but no shirt.

'Morning is the best part of the day. How are you feeling?'

'Lousy. Just what I need, a broken arm to start a new job with. I can't drive, I can't write.' He was not in a sunny mood, and she couldn't blame him.

'We'll manage. Tomorrow there are two more drivers coming for interviews. Maybe one of them will be the right one for us.'

He grunted something unintelligible and leaned back in his chair.

'Would you like some coffee? Some more aspirin?'

'Coffee would be nice. I just had some aspirin.'

Megan went into the kitchen. It wasn't any better than the one she would have once the Ingrams had left the house. Nick had hired a woman to do his cleaning and cooking, but she wouldn't start until Monday. So far they had managed on their own, eating mostly eggs, fruits and vegetables she bought at the local *pasar*.

'I'll fix us some breakfast,' she said when she offered him his coffee. 'Scrambled eggs and toast all right? Or are you getting tired of that?'

'It's fine.' He stared gloomily out over the glorious green landscape, too preoccupied to enjoy it.

She brought the food out on the porch and they ate in silence, Nick awkwardly forking the eggs with his left hand.

'Where did you leave the car?'

'On Jalan Surapati, about a block from the Horizon.'

'I'll go get it.'

'No, you won't. I'll send a driver to get it on Monday afternoon.'

'That's nonsense. I can do it today. Nothing else to do, anyway. And I don't like the idea of sitting here without a car. I'll get a taxi or a *bemo* into town and I can be back in a couple of hours.'

He gave her an exasperated look. 'Megan, you haven't yet driven here, you're not familiar with that car, and you don't speak the language.'

'Oh, for heaven's sake, stop treating me like a child! I've been other places where I didn't speak the local language. I manage! I'm very creative that way. I can drive that car! I can drive on the left side of the road! I've been sitting next to you for days. It doesn't feel strange any more. I've got to start some time!'

'But not in Denpasar, dammit!' protested Nick.

'It's Sunday. The traffic will be light. And will you *please* credit me with some brains and some common sense? Will you *please* credit me for not being stupid? What is it with you, anyway? What makes you think I can't do a simple thing like driving a car back home?'

He shrugged. 'Never mind.'

'No! Don't never mind me! You'd better not keep doing

this sort of thing to me. I came to Bali to do a job, not to be babysat by you!'

Nick's mouth quirked. '*Touché.*'

She got up and stacked the plates. 'And now I'm going to the kitchen to wash the dishes,' she said between clenched teeth. 'But only because you're incapacitated. It's your turn today.'

His smile deepened. 'I'm so glad you're staying with me,' he said. 'Now you can take care of me.'

'Whooptie doo!'

The dishes done, she went back to him. 'I want the keys,' she demanded, holding out her hand. He gave her a long, hard stare, and she stared back at him just as hard.

'I can stand here as long as it takes,' she informed him.

'I believe you can.'

'Where are the keys?' she persisted.

'You're quite determined.'

'I thought I made that clear.'

He sighed. 'All right, then. The keys are in my bedroom, on the dresser.'

'Thank you.'

'Don't have any flat tyres.'

'Wouldn't you like that!'

'I'm just worried about you taking off with Robert Redford and forgetting about me.'

'Hah!'

Megan walked into the village to find a ride. The best she could do was a *bemo*, a small van with two wooden benches built in lengthwise at the back, facing each other. It was not the most comfortable mode of transportation, but the fare was a pittance and she watched her companions with interest. A couple of young men, a mother with a baby, an old crone without a tooth in her mouth and two chickens in a cage on her lap.

She found the Mitsubishi without any trouble. She climbed

in and examined the map, then started the car and drove down the street and out of town, tracing her way back home. The road was narrow and led through small villages and past ancient Hindu temples. The traffic was light on this Sunday morning and she enjoyed the trip.

She was back home an hour later, finding Nick still on the veranda, reading.

'So, you made it,' he greeted her.

'So I did. No accidents, no minor scratches or dents, no flat tyres. Are you disappointed?' she asked lightly.

'Don't be nasty.'

She ignored that. 'How's your arm?'

'Could be worse.'

'That's a good way to look at it. Be positive.'

He gave her a disgusted look. 'Miss Cheerful!'

'Somebody better be cheerful around here, or we'll both drown in gloom. This is Bali, remember? Paradise on earth. Tribes of tourists flock to the beaches to enjoy it, depleting their bank accounts for the trip or going into debt for the next five years.'

'They don't have a job to do and they don't have a broken arm,' he said morosely.

'If you're going to sit here and feel sorry for yourself and make me totally depressed in the process, I'm leaving.'

'Oh, please!' He managed a grin. 'I'm helpless. Don't leave—I'll be good.'

'Promise?'

He nodded, face solemn. 'Promise.'

It was not a promise easily kept over the next few weeks. He had a hate affair going with his cast, calling it unprintable names. His mood was foul. Megan couldn't really blame him. To feel so confined and handicapped wasn't easy for anybody, and most certainly not for a man of Nick's temperament. To have to ask her for help all the time wasn't easy. Megan tried to ignore his bad moods, but she was sorely tested. She had her own problems, trying to settle down in the job, figuring out what to do and where to start.

She was delighted when they received an invitation to a farewell party for the Ingrams. She was looking forward to meeting some of the other people in the foreign community.

They seemed a cheerful group, of various nationalities, and they all seemed to know each other quite well. The party was quite a rowdy affair, with a number of bawdy toasts and speeches to the departing family.

'Ah, the new face in town!'

Megan looked up. The man next to her scrutinised her slowly as he extended his right hand. He had sandy-brown hair, interesting green eyes and a cocky grin, exposing strong white teeth.

'I'm Peter Strauss. Pleased to meet you.'

'I'm Megan Opperman.'

'I know.'

She smiled. 'News gets around.'

He nodded. 'Fast!' His tone was dry. 'You're here with the new housing project.'

'Right.'

'Attention, attention!' someone shouted. 'Will Mr Nick Donovan and Ms Megan Opperman please come forward!'

Megan cocked an eyebrow. 'What's this?'

Peter shrugged and followed her as she moved to the front of the room, where Nick was already standing, talking to Brian Williams, a corpulent, cigar-smoking New Zealander in a flowered Hawaiian shirt.

'We call him the Sultan,' Peter informed her in a whisper. 'He's sort of the self-appointed leader of the foreign community here.'

The Sultan grabbed her hand, took out his cigar and smiled at her. 'Welcome, Miss Opperman. Stand here, please.' He positioned her next to Nick.

'Ladies and gentlemen!' he shouted. 'May I introduce to

you our two good-looking American newcomers! They truly are an asset to our community. Look at them! Don't they make a gorgeous pair?' There was a round of enthusiastic applause. Nick's left arm came around her shoulders and he grinned at her suggestively. She went rigid with resentment and barely managed a smile in response for the benefit of the audience.

'*He* says he's her boss,' the Sultan went on. '*She* says she works for him. Now, do you believe that's all there is to it? Then you're dumber than I thought! They're living in the same house—what does that tell you?' Loud laughter and big grins in their direction followed his remark. Megan, stiff and self-conscious, smiled till her jaws ached, feeling like a fool. Great, she thought, just what I need.

'Megan and Nick, we wish you welcome to our little but happy community! May Bali inspire your hearts, warm your souls and give you joy!'

Again everybody applauded and called out greetings of welcome. There was a small pause while the man caught his breath and took a puff from his smelly cigar. 'Now I have an announcement! We are going to have our singing contest . . .'

Megan heard no more. With the attention diverted from the two of them, she turned to Nick and glared at him as she shook off his arm. 'That wasn't exactly necessary, was it?'

'What wasn't?' he asked, looking innocent.

'You didn't need to reinforce that fool's insinuations by putting your arm around me!'

His eyes sparked with laughter. 'Meggie, loosen up, will you? It's all in fun, you know.'

'Maybe for you.' She turned away from him and found Peter at her side again.

He looked at the empty glass in her hand. 'How about another drink?'

'Please.'

'What were you drinking?'

'I have no idea. The bartender's special, I believe.'

Peter rolled his eyes. 'You put Keith behind a bar and he starts being creative. You never know what you'll end up with. It's a miracle, truly. The man is an accountant, if you can believe that.' He took her glass. 'I'll see what we can do. Come along.' He took her hand and grinned. 'Don't want to lose you in this crowd.'

The crowd was all of thirty people, but Megan did not protest as he drew her along to the bar, where he parked her on a stool, and stood close by her as he talked to the man named Keith behind the bar. He was a greying Canadian in his forties, and looked as if he was inviting a coronary with his beefy build.

'Another one of your magic potions for the lady,' Peter ordered.

She watched as the man assembled the drink—a dab of this, a drop of that—making quite a show of it.

'Mmm, good,' she said, taking a sip. Keith looked pleased.

'So, what do you do on Bali?' she asked Peter.

'I'm an adviser at a technical school. I help with developing a curriculum, setting up classes, buying equipment, that sort of thing.'

'You're German?'

'Right.'

They talked for a while, about his work, her work, life on Bali.

'What about this Nick Donovan?' he asked. 'You live with him?'

'For the time being. I'm getting the Ingrams' house.'

'I see. Forgive me for being so forward, but is he your boss, or is there more?'

'You *are* being forward.'

He grinned disarmingly. 'Don't want to get into trouble. I like to know the score before I plunge myself head first into a new romance.'

'You've known me twenty minutes!'

'Oh, for me, it doesn't take long,' he said, quasi-serious. 'I'm German.'

She took another sip from her drink. 'I don't picture the Germans as great romantics.'

'No? What about Heinrich Heine, Richard Wagner?'

'They're a bit old now.'

He laughed. 'True! But you didn't answer my question. Anything going on between you and Donovan?'

'He's my boss.'

'Only?'

She nodded. 'Only.' Liar, she told herself. Well, what was she supposed to do? Tell this stranger she'd once had a long and passionate affair with Nick, and was still struggling with the aftershocks? It would be all over the island in a matter of hours.

'Good.' He gave her a blissful smile and put a possessive arm around her shoulder.

One thing led to another. He invited her to come to the beach with him the next day. Megan said no, she had other things to do, maybe another time. She wasn't sure that going to a Bali beach with a German Don Juan was a good idea. He begged. He pleaded. She gave in. The beach really did beckon, she had to admit. Three weeks in Bali and she hadn't seen the ocean yet. It was unheard-of.

She saw Nick talking with the Ingrams, but his blue eyes were on her. Every time she looked in his direction, she met his eyes. It was hard to keep her attention directed at Peter, who was telling her an involved story about some corruption scheme he had uncovered. He was rather proud of himself, but she was less than interested. Nick's eyes were boring holes in her back.

A tall blonde appeared at their side. 'Is this man monopolising you? Keeping you captive? Boring you?' she asked Megan.

'Hello, Pam,' Peter said. 'Nasty as ever, I can tell.'

'I just feel sorry for the poor girl. You can make it hard on us women, you know.'

'Pam to the rescue,' he said sarcastically, and she laughed. She turned to Megan and extended her hand.

'Hi, I'm Pam McGregor. You'd better watch out with him,' she advised, thumbing in Peter's direction. 'He consumes women like salted peanuts.'

'I think I can handle him,' Megan told her.

'I wish you luck.' Pam threw Peter a teasing smile and he glowered back at her.

'Get lost, Pammy, or I'll tell Tony about you.'

Pam laughed. 'Oh, boy, now I'm in trouble! OK, OK, I'm leaving. There's Tony waving at me. He wants to go. Oh, by the way, Megan,' she said, pointing at Tony, 'that one's mine.'

Megan laughed. 'OK, I'll remember.' As Pam left, she turned back to Peter and studied his face. 'So you're a heart-breaker?'

'Don't listen to Pam. Let me get you another drink.'

'I've had enough, thank you.'

It was getting late and she was just considering going home when Nick materialised at her side.

'Let's go home,' he suggested. It sounded rather proprietorial, as if she was supposed to move when he did. She let it pass.

'All right.' She looked at Peter, who had stuck to her side all evening. 'Have you met Nick Donovan?'

The two men shook hands, sizing each other up.

'All right, let's go,' said Nick, putting his left hand on Megan's upper arm.

'If you'd like to stay, I can take you home later,' Peter suggested, and Nick threw him a murderous look.

'She's coming with me,' he stated flatly.

Megan didn't like the sound of it, not one bit, but she'd talk to him later.

'I want to go now, Peter. I'll see you tomorrow.'

'Fine. I'll pick you up at eight.'

The night was warm and balmy and full of mysterious sounds. They walked silently for some time, then Megan stepped in front of Nick to make him stop.

'What is the matter with you?' she demanded.

'The matter with me? Nothing. What are you talking about?'

'I didn't like your earlier performance, and now this! "Let's go home. She's coming with me," ' she mimicked. 'I didn't like the sound of that. You don't tell me what to do, and you don't need to answer my questions for me.'

'I was only coming to the rescue. The guy was sticking to you like a piece of bubble gum.'

'So what if he was? Maybe I liked it! At any rate, it's none of your business, is it? I can take care of myself. I can take care of sticky men. I don't need your help, OK?'

'If you say so.'

'I say so! I'm sick and tired of your interference in my life! You seem to have trouble remembering that you're only my boss! We may be sharing the same office and the same house, and we're spending a lot of time with each other, but I would like to remind you that . . .'

'Shut up.' His left arm came around her like a band of steel, pulling her against his side, and his mouth descended on hers with forceful possession. He kissed her with a hard, barely contained passion, demanding response. Megan's fury was soon overpowered by a treacherous, giddy desire sweeping through her. She felt dizzy and hot and out of control, her knees and legs trembling with weakness. Her mouth answered to his, and her arms went around him to steady herself as she gave herself up to the sensations flooding her.

Then he let her go. 'Don't fool yourself,' he said quietly, and the words seemed to reach her through a thick fog. 'Don't pretend there's nothing between us, because there is,

Megan. You can't fight it. The only question is, what are we going to do about it?'

She stared at him in the dark. His face was full of shadows. She hated him. She hated herself.

'You bastard,' she whispered. 'You miserable, rotten bastard!' A sob broke from her, then another. She took a step back, turned and ran off, stumbling on the uneven road surface.

'Megan!'

She ran on blindly, not stopping until she reached the house. The door wasn't locked. She went inside, into her room and closed the door. There was no key, no lock.

She threw herself on the bed, tears streaming down her face. 'Oh, God,' she moaned, 'I can't take this any more!'

The tension between them was growing progressively worse. And it wasn't hate or anger or fear, no matter what it seemed on the outside. The feelings were what they had always been and they were very close to the surface, but finding very different expressions now—irritations, verbal battles, silly arguments.

Megan moaned in helpless despair. Nick still wanted her. She still wanted him. It showed itself in an innocent gesture, a glance, a sudden memory triggered by a careless word, like puffs of volcanic heat rising to the surface, indicating a greater pressure buried below, waiting to explode.

She could not give into it. She had to hold it in, tie it up, lock it up . . . and sometimes she was bursting with it, the tension pressing behind her eyes, her forehead, her fingers trembling with it.

There was a knock on the door. 'Megan?'

'Go away!'

Nick entered the room and sat down on the side of her bed.

'I said go away!' Her voice was muffled by the pillow. She dared not look up. 'Can't I have my privacy? Do you always have to come barging in on me?'

'Sit up, Megan. Let's talk.'

'No!'

His left arm was in fine shape. He took her shoulder and turned her on her back. She threw her arm across her face, but there was no hiding from him. She hated it. She hated feeling what she was feeling. She hated him.

'I hate you,' she whispered thickly.

'No, you don't. You feel what I feel, and it isn't hate.'

'So you can look in my head now, can you?' she asked fiercely, her body stiff with anger and resentment.

'To a degree, yes. I know you pretty well, Megan.'

She clenched her hands into fists. 'You only think you do. And what is it you feel that I'm supposed to feel? Lust? Animal passion?'

'Let's talk, instead of argue.'

'There's nothing to talk about! All you want is to get me back in your bed. Ever since we started this job together! I'm not stupid, you know! I'm not blind! Well, you can forget it!'

'I've tried.' His voice was low and quiet.

'Try harder! There's no way, no way in the world I'm going to have another affair with you just so you can dump me again once the job is finished.'

'You're not being fair, Megan.'

She scooted into a sitting position and glared at him. 'Fair? Look who's talking about *fair*!'

His eyes were bleak. 'You'll never forgive me, will you?'

She looked away. 'Probably not,' she said coldly.

CHAPTER SIX

'MEGAN,' said Nick after a pause, 'I'd like us to try and be friends. Apart from everything else, we used to be pretty good friends. Let's make a new start, get to know each other again.'

'I don't want a new start.'

There was a silence.

'Can we try to be friends?' His eyes locked hers. 'You think that's asking too much?'

'It doesn't seem realistic to me,' she said stiffly.

His mouth slanted into a smile. 'About as realistic as we can be, unless we want to cuddle up at night. And I don't believe we're quite ready for that.'

I'm not ready for that!'

'Maybe I'm not, either.'

She gave him a scornful look. 'Hah!'

Nick studied her for a moment. 'Speaking on a strictly physical level, Megan, I doubt my desires are any more intense than yours.'

'That's what you want to believe.'

'I'm neither blind nor dumb, Megan.'

No, he wasn't. She'd loved him once—it was hard not to remember that. It was hard not to remember all the nights they'd shared a bed, all the times they'd made love. She turned her head away. She didn't want to look at him, knowing he was right there at the edge of her bed. All she had to do was reach out a hand and touch him.

'Go away,' she said, and her voice sounded strange.

He came to his feet slowly. 'Friends?' he asked quietly.

Megan nodded silently, not looking at him. Friends. She

didn't know how they were going to accomplish it, but it was better than being enemies.

She heard him move across the room, then the door opened and closed.

Megan sat on the beach and let the sun warm her skin, sipping an over-sugared and under-cooled Coke bought from one of the vendors haunting the beach. A number of them had already come by, trying to sell her sea shells, embroidered dresses, crocheted bikinis, small black carvings, junk jewellery. She peered out over the glittering water. Peter was out in the waves somewhere, body surfing. He'd tried to teach her without much success and she'd come out, exhausted, to bake some more in the sun.

'Massage? You want massage?' Two little old ladies wearing sarongs and conical hats looked at her hopefully, each carrying a can of coconut oil in her hand.

'*Tidak, terima kasih*. No, thank you.'

'Is nice. I give you special. Ony one thousand rupiahs.'

Megan shook her head. '*Tidak mau.*' She'd just watched a topless Aussie girl being massaged not thirty feet from her, and her body was now gleaming with oil. Megan wasn't ready for the experience. Maybe she was a prude, but her liberation hadn't progressed to the point where she was ready to take off her bikini top and have a wrinkled old lady knead her every inch on a public beach.

Peter was plodding through the sand towards her, water glittering on his skin. He was lean and muscled and brown, a healthy-looking specimen, masculine and virile, yet he didn't do a thing for her, caused no secret stirrings in her blood. He dropped the surfboard in the sand and showered water all over her. He glanced at the women, then grinned down at Megan.

'Having a massage?' he enquired.

'No. I told them, but they won't leave.'

'Oh, go ahead. It feels good.'

'I don't want to,' she said firmly.

'Why not? Afraid to take your bikini top off?' He was laughing at her. 'You Americans are really something! For all your supposed modernism, progressiveness and liberation, there's a lot of puritanism left in you. No nudity on TV, no models wearing bras on commercials. So repressive! Not a healthy attitude, if you ask me.'

She smiled sweetly. 'Nobody asked you.'

'What's wrong with a normal display of the human body—in context, of course?'

'Bodies are private, personal property. Maybe what we Americans have is discretion, a sense of propriety.'

'A sense of propriety?' Peter laughed indulgently. 'OK, if that's the way you want to look at it.' He took his towel and began to rub himself dry.

'You know what, Peter?' she asked sunnily. 'You're an arrogant son of a bitch.'

'Tut, tut. Not very proper, calling people names.'

She ignored that and turned over on her stomach, lowering her head on her arms and closing her eyes. He plopped down next to her on his bamboo beach mat. 'Are you angry?'

'Angry? With you? I wouldn't waste my energy.'

'Good. What do you say we have some lunch?'

A shadow fell over them. 'Peter! Hello!'

Megan raised her head and looked up. A tall blonde in a one-piece black swim-suit towered over them. Pam, she realised. 'Hello, Pam,' she said.

'Oh! Megan!' Pam laughed. 'I didn't recognise you seeing just your back. But I should have known. Peter never wastes much time, does he?'

Peter looked at her darkly. 'Where's Tony?'

'Over there, buying another beach mat. This one has had it.' She gestured at the one rolled up and tucked under her arm. 'We were just going out for some lunch. Why don't you two join us?'

'I'd like that,' Megan answered, seeing Tony loping towards them through the sand. He seemed all arms and legs, and was painfully thin.

They ate in one of the small open-air restaurants that lined the road. Tables were set out amid a profusion of large plants and cages of exotic songbirds. In the shade of the trees, the air was cooler, a welcome relief from the blistering sun on the beach. Megan inspected her arms, hoping she wasn't getting a sunburn.

Pam was talkative and amusing, digging at Peter, who was not short on comebacks and not at all hampered by the fact that English was not his mother tongue. Megan suspected that at some point the two had had a short but explosive relationship. Tony, a studious-looking Scotsman, was rather quiet, but every time he did open his mouth he produced a witticism that had them all laughing till their sides hurt.

By the time Megan got home, late in the afternoon, she did have a distinct rosy-warm feeling all over her, despite the use of tanning lotion. She found Nick on the veranda, reading an impressive-looking document. Even on Sunday he was working.

'Looks like you had a good time,' Nick commented. There was a hint of mockery in his voice as he looked her over.

'Yes, I did.' She met his eyes in challenge. She knew him well enough to be aware that he hadn't liked her going out with Peter; the little telltale signs didn't elude her. 'I tried to body surf, but I didn't show a lot of talent in that direction. We had lunch in one of those little places by the beach. I had fried turtle. Ever had that?'

'Yes.' He frowned. 'You've got quite a burn. A definite shade of boiled lobster, I'd say. Didn't you use lotion?'

'Of course I did, and it's not that bad.'

'It looks bad enough. You'd better get something on it.'

'I will, Doctor, I will. I'll go take a shower, and then

I'll fix us something to eat.' Sunday was Ibu's day off. Ibu was in her fifties, tiny and strong, coming to work each day wearing the traditional sarong, with her black hair tied back in a bun. Not a grey hair was evident, and Megan wondered if she dyed it.

'Don't bother about dinner. We can try out Murni's Warung,' Nick suggested.

'Good idea.' Apart from a variety of Indonesian dishes, Murni's Warung also boasted 'Authentic American Upper Elk Valley Hamburgers' and 'The Best Chocolate Chip Cookies East of San Francisco'. Megan had never heard of Upper Elk Valley hamburgers.

'If you need help putting lotion on your back, let me know,' he called after her.

'I can manage,' she returned automatically.

But of course she couldn't; there was no way she could reach all of her back. She stared at herself in the mirror and shrugged. Oh, well, maybe it wouldn't matter. She dressed in a thin cotton dress and found Nick in the kitchen, pouring himself a drink.

'Would you like some sherry?' he asked.

'I'll have some soda water with some lime in it. I feel dehydrated.'

'You are, no doubt. You didn't need help putting cream on your back?'

'It's all right,' she said lightly.

'From what I can see, your back looks worse than the rest. Don't be silly, Megan.'

She gave him a saccharine smile. 'Shut up, Nick.'

But it wasn't all right. She woke up in the middle of the night and couldn't get back to sleep. Cursing herself for her stupidity, she put more lotion on her arms and legs and front, but her burning back prevented her from falling asleep again. Every time she moved, it hurt. In exasperation, she got up and got in the shower, letting cool water run over her back. It

felt good while it lasted. Once out of the shower, it hurt worse
than ever.

There was a knock on her door. 'Megan, are you all right?'

'I'm fine!'

'May I come in?'

'No!' She was sitting naked on the bed. Even wearing a
nightgown was uncomfortable; it seemed to trap the heat
radiating from her skin.

Apparently not taking no for an answer, Nick opened her
door and stepped inside.

'I said no!' She grabbed the sheet and pulled it to her.

'Don't be stupid, Meggie. I heard the shower. It's your
back, isn't it?'

She closed her eyes briefly. 'Yes.'

'I'll put something on it. I promise you I won't rape or
ravish you. I've got this.' He showed her a bottle of lotion. 'It's
very good. It has a local anaesthetic in it.'

She stared at the bottle, not answering.

'You don't want me to touch you, I understand that. Every
time I touch you, my hormones go on a stampede. It's a
problem, I realise. But I'll be very fast and I'll do my very best
not to have lustful thoughts while I'm looking at your baked
back.'

'Very funny! Oh, go ahead!' She turned on to her stomach,
pulling the sheet up to her waist.

'Good girl.' Nick pulled the sheet a little lower.

'That's enough!'

He laughed softly. 'I want to get it all.' He squirted some of
the lotion on to her burning back and she yelped.

'It's cold!'

'Should feel good.' He began to smooth the cool lotion over
her hot flesh with gentle, rhythmic strokes, working it into the
skin. Megan clamped her jaws shut, but after a moment she
began to relax.

It felt heavenly. Too heavenly. Yet she couldn't blame

him, or could she? He wasn't doing anything out of the ordinary, or was he? He moved his hands across her back, over her shoulders and back down, yet the sensuous touch of the movements made the blood rush hot through her veins.

'You've got a line,' he commented. 'Why didn't you take off your top?'

'Because I didn't want to.' Her voice was muffled by the pillow. 'I'm a prudish, puritanical American, and I had that discussion already once today.'

'I bet,' he said drily. 'That Strauss is a fast mover. He was ready to see you take it all off.'

'Just because *you* think that way, it doesn't . . .'

Nick laughed, his hand still moving sensuously over her back. 'Don't be naïve, darling.'

'Don't darling me! And what makes you think Peter is a fast mover?'

'One look at him. I'm surprised you were home so early.'

As a matter of fact, it hadn't easy. But by four she'd had enough of sea, sun and Strauss, and had demanded he bring her home, which eventually he had done, but not without her getting angry first.

'You don't like him, do you?' queried Megan.

'Not particularly.'

'Why?' She turned her head and peeped at him through her lashes, in a way grateful for the distraction of conversation. His hand was the hand of a lover, not of some anonymous person doing someone else a favour.

He shrugged. 'He just rubs me the wrong way.'

Because Peter is interested in me, that's why, she said to herself. But she knew better than to point that out. She didn't like Nick having those proprietorial feelings for her, but there was little she could do about it.

'This should do it.' His hand left her back and she was almost sorry.

'Thanks.' She closed her eyes, feeling sleepy and almost

relaxed, but not quite. Not as long as he was in the room. Then she felt his hand on her hair and she tensed instantly. His mouth was suddenly close to her ear.

'Goodnight, Megan.' She felt his lips below her ear, a soft, gentle touch, and her heart began to gallop.

'Don't do that!' she whispered fiercely.

'Nothing but a friendly goodnight kiss,' he said softly, and she heard the smile in his voice. He straightened away from her. She heard his footsteps across the room, then the opening and closing of the door.

After the Ingrams had left the island, Megan packed her suitcases and moved into the house, welcomed by a smiling Ariaso. The first thing Megan noticed was a large vase of flowers on the living-room table, with a note leaning up against it. 'Welcome to your happy home away from home!' she read. 'Come have dinner with me tonight. Pam.' Megan smiled and took her luggage to the bedroom. She made a tour of the house, finding everything clean and in order until she got to the kitchen.

There was no refrigerator. The space it had occupied was conspicuously empty. On closer inspection, she also found the big standing fan missing in the living-room. Ariaso, waving her hands, tried to explain to her what had happened, and Megan caught something about men in a big car who had taken them away, but her knowledge of Indonesian did not get her as far as to understand the who and the why.

'You think you'll like the house?' Pam asked her when she arrived for the promised dinner that night.

Megan looked around with interest. Pam had done an interesting job decorating her house, using local materials—baskets and batik cushions and local art on the walls.

'I'd like it a lot better with a fridge and a fan.'

Pam grimaced. 'Oh, boy! I think I know what happened.

David Ingram worked for the Ministry of Agriculture. I bet they bought them for him and then took them away after he left.'

'Well, somehow I'll have to get new ones.'

'There's no fridge in the kitchen and no fan in the living-room,' she told Nick the next morning. 'I checked with the Ministry, and from what I gather they belonged to the Ministry of Agriculture, so they took them away.'

He closed his eyes wearily. 'Great. God, I hate this stuff! All these petty little things drive me straight up the wall.'

'I understand that,' she acknowledged calmly, 'but they promised us a fully furnished house. They'll have to get me a fridge and a fan.'

He grimaced. 'Sounds simple enough, doesn't it? Well, it isn't. We've got our supposedly fully furnished houses. The local budget doesn't cover furniture, there's no money for it.'

'Then they'll have to figure out something else! I've got to have a fridge! And I hardly think a fan is a luxury item here, either!'

Nick looked at her irritably. 'Don't argue with me. I *agree*. The only thing you're wrong about is that *they* don't have to figure out anything. They won't. I'm the one who's going to have to deal with this. Find the money somehow. Fiddle with the budget. Get somebody interested. And I haven't got the time or the inclination for it, but I'll see what I can do.'

'Thanks,' she said through tight lips. 'I'm sorry to bother you, but you are the project director and you're the one I have to approach.' She turned and walked out.

Two weeks later there was no progress. Nick was irritable every time she mentioned the subject. 'I've got better things to do than chase a damn refrigerator!' he exploded one day. 'I told you I'm dealing with it! Now, will you relax and wait, for God's sake?'

Fury overwhelmed her. He had better things to do than worry about her comfort, did he? She was just being a nuisance, was she? All right, she'd take care of the issue once and for all! She took the car, drove into Denpasar, bought a fan and a small refrigerator with her own money and drove them back herself in the back of the car.

When she arrived at the office the next morning, Nick was already there, engrossed in his work.

'I've got a fridge and a fan,' she announced without preliminaries, 'so you can drop the subject. I won't bother you again and I won't take your precious time any more.'

He looked up from his work and straightened in his chair, his face an open question. 'You what? How did you do that?'

She squared her shoulders and looked directly at him. 'I went to the bank in Denpasar, withdrew money from my own account, went to the store and bought the fan and fridge. When I leave here, I'll sell them again and the difference will be my loss. So let's please forget about it, because I'm tired of the whole damned subject.'

Nick swore under his breath. 'After all the work I put in trying to get the blasted things, you go out and *buy* them?'

'I was tired of waiting!'

'And I'm tired of wasting my time!'

'Well, I'm sorry! There's no making you happy, is there? It's damned if I do and damned if I don't! It wasn't *my* fault the Ministry blew it! It wasn't *my* fault there's no money for furniture in the budget! It's not *my* fault that you're the one who got saddled with the job of dealing with it. I *know* the bureaucracy is impossible to deal with, so I thought I'd find my own solution. Now you think what you want and do what you want, I don't care!' She grabbed her briefcase from the chair, slammed the door behind her and rushed out of the building. She found Atjin, the driver, waiting for her by the Toyota, lounging lazily against the door and smoking a clove cigarette.

He drove her to the flood village, where she had a meeting with the people who were on her list to be allocated the new houses. She would have to organise them into a co-op, find out what they needed in their new houses, visit some of their existing homes. She was gone all day, and went staight home afterwards.

She was in the living-room, changing the plug on her favourite reading-lamp she'd brought with her from home, when she heard a knock on the screen door.

'Megan? It's me, Nick.'

'Come in.'

'What the hell are you doing?' he asked, the moment he entered.

'Changing a plug, can't you see?'

'With a *paring knife?*'

She shrugged. 'I don't have a screwdriver.'

He rolled his eyes. 'You know I have one. Why didn't you come and borrow it?'

'This knife works fine.' The idea of borrowing his screwdriver had occurred to her, of course, but she'd seen enough of him for one day and rejected the idea. 'See? All done.' She held up the plug triumphantly, then inserted it in the wall outlet and bright light flooded the room.

'I'm impressed,' he said drily.

'Didn't think I could do that, did you?' Her eyes challenged him.

'Well . . . to tell you the truth, knowing you don't know how to change a tyre, I naturally assumed you wouldn't know how to change a plug.'

'Naturally,' she agreed sarcastically.

'So, what's next?' Your mixer, the stereo?'

She narrowed her eyes. 'You're a louse, you know that?' she siad, her tone mild. 'And no, I wouldn't change the plug on my mixer, if I'd brought one. I'd get a transformer. And a stereo has to have the same cycles or it won't work properly, transformer or no. Why are you trying to catch me? See how stupid I really am?'

'You know your electricity,' said Nick, and the old familiar grin began to spread over his face. She wasn't going to be taken in with it this time.

'Why did you come here?' she demanded.

His eyes held hers, provoking. 'My instincts told me you were in mortal danger.'

She smiled sweetly. 'Your instincts are as lousy as the rest of you.'

'You're doing wonders for my ego.'

She ignored that. 'Why did you come here?' she repeated.

'Just wanting to see how your day was in mud village.'

She lifted a disbelieving eyebrow. 'You could have asked me that tomorrow at the office.'

His grin deepened. 'I also wanted to apologise for my bad temper about your refrigerator and fan. I'm sorry I'm so unbearable about that sort of thing.'

'Anything else?' she asked coolly.

'You look like a stuffy schoolmarm. Do you accept my apology?'

'All right, I suppose I will.'

'Smile!' ordered Nick.

'I don't feel like smiling,' she lied. It was hard to keep a straight face when he looked at her with those laughing eyes, taunting her.

'Yes, you do.'

'Oh, stop it!' She began to laugh. No matter how she sometimes resented their appeal, she'd never been able to resist those eyes.

'Good, that's better. Now, there is something else. I wanted to remind you that my cast is coming off tomorrow and to make sure you'll be there for the meeting at two, in case I don't make it back in time.'

'I'll be there,' she reassured him.

'If I have time, I'll stop at the supermarket. Anything you need?'

She smiled at him. 'Yes, rat poison.'

'You have any rats?'

'Just one big one. And he keeps coming back. Sits right there in that chair and makes me mad.'

His eyes gleamed, the humour not contained. 'I'd give him a double dose, if I were you,' he said softly.

'He deserves it.'

'You're probably right.' He got up and walked over to the door. 'I think I'll go.' He sighed melodramatically. 'I'm obviously not very welcome.'

'Oh, sure you are,' she said in a soothing tone. 'Sit down, darling. I'll fix us a drink.'

'Thank you,' he said gravely. 'I'd like that.'

The next day, Nick returned from the hospital just as the meeting was starting. He entered the room quietly and sat down across from Megan, grinning at her as he lifted his arm for her to see.

After the meeting, they went back into their office.

'I'm a whole man again,' Nick said with satisfaction, holding out both his arms in front of him.

'Congratulations.'

He moved toward her across the room. 'I'd like to try them out.'

'Oh? What did you have in mind?'

'Come a little closer,' he invited.

'I don't think that's a good idea.'

'Why not?'

'It sounds dangerous. I don't trust you. I don't trust that look in your eyes.'

He straightened his face into a mask of solemn sincerity. 'My intentions are completely honourable. Just a friendly hug, a brotherly hug. Just to see if I can still do it.'

'You've never been able to give me hugs of the friendly, brotherly variety. Why would you start now?'

'Because that's all that's allowed, isn't it?'

'Nick . . .'

His arms slid around her. He held her carefully, like a china doll, as if afraid he'd break her.

Megan's heart began to race. Her face was nearly touching his shirt. She smelled the warm, familiar scent of him. Warning bells roared in her head, yet she didn't draw away.

'How's that?' he said.

'I've never had a hug like this,' she said.

'Not even from your brother?'

Megan closed her eyes and laughed. Her brother gave her bear hugs that nearly crushed her.

'No, not even from my brother.'

'You'll have to teach me how to do it, then.'

'I don't think that's necessary. Your arms are working just fine. You'd better let go.'

Nick's chin dropped into her hair. 'You really want me to?' he whispered.

'Yes,' she said, but her voice was unsteady. It was a lie, a blatant lie. She wanted his arms around her. She wanted him to hold her and kiss her. The yearning was suddenly so strong that she closed her eyes and clenched her hands, which lay against his chest.

'No, you don't. His mouth moved to her temple, and his arms drew her closer against him. She didn't resist, and his mouth moved softly down her cheek until it reached her lips.

Her blood pounded in her head and breathing was suddenly difficult. Nick's lips were firm and warm on hers, and she had no strength to avert her face, but stood unmoving in his embrace, with her hands on his chest, like a barrier between them.

Soon the kiss, careful as it had started, was no longer tentative and gentle, but a hungry, urgent searching that drained her of all will to resist, stirring in her wild and primitive desires that obliterated all reason.

He slipped his hands forward, took her wrists and extracted her hands which were caught between them, lifting them around his neck. Then his arms slid down to her hips and pressed her closer against him, while all along his mouth, open and searching, tantalised her senses. Her blood sang, and her body went limp and weightless.

A loud thump against the window crashed into their oblivion. They drew apart, staring at each other in stunned silence, their breathing hard and laboured.

'What was that?' asked Megan, her voice husky.

'A bird, probably. It flew against the window.'

Megan took a shaky step backward. 'Poor bird.' *Poor me*, she added silently, swallowing hard.

She was back in the drab little office with the smudgy walls and the worn linoleum. She looked at Nick. Oh, damn, she thought, why does he do this to me? I don't want these cheap snatches of passion—in a hotel bathroom, on the edge of his bed, in this shabby office. So why can't I resist him?

She took a deep breath, trying to clear her head. 'I'd better get some work done,' she said, picking up a file from her desk in an effort to look casual.

'Don't be mad at me,' said Nick, and the smile was back in his eyes, pleading with her. 'I couldn't help myself. You know how it is with me—I can't keep my animal urges under control. It's a cross, truly.'

She looked away. Her throat closed up, and treacherous tears burned behind her eyes. She didn't reply and there was a moment of heavy silence.

'I guess you were right, after all,' he said then, and there was an odd tone in his voice now. 'I've never been able to give you hugs of the friendly, brotherly variety. I suppose I never will be.'

'Oh, go away,' she muttered. 'Go try your arms out on somebody else!'

* * *

The weeks went by. Weeks of long days, full of
work—research and problem solving, meetings with
government officials and villagers, trips to other villages. Their
relationship seemed to have improved. It was easier now that
Megan was living in her own house. The conflicts and
disagreements were confined to the work situation—arguments
about the housing designs, about major and minor affairs.
What materials to use in the construction—local clay tile or
asbestos from Jakarta; what to use for walls—local brick or
imported wallboard.

Yet neither was fooled by the supposedly relaxed
atmosphere. She wondered how long it would take before she
would really feel at ease around Nick.

She made new friends, went for drinks to people's houses, to
dinner parties and games evenings where she played cards or
mah-jong. Every Saturday she played volley ball, as did Nick.
There were weekends on the beach, and dinners at small local
restaurants by the roadside, where the fish was fresh and the
beer cold.

She had not encouraged Peter, who seemed hell-bent on
seducing her, and eventually he had taken up with a gorgeous
Balinese schoolteacher with seductive eyes and an innocent
smile.

She went to the local galleries and art shops, and learned
about Balinese painting and wood carving. She visited the
ancient Hindu temples, and the traditional festivals and
ceremonies with all the glamour and glitter of elaborate
costumes and masks and music. She tried to immerse herself in
the local culture, tried to occupy her mind with new ideas and
concepts.

And through all this frantic activity Nick would not leave
her mind. He seemed ever present, not only at work, but in
her off hours as well. His face haunted her. The look in his
eyes—the look she sometimes noticed when she caught him off
guard. It was a most disturbing expression in the bright blue

eyes, and she tried to ignore it.

The longing for what she'd once had was still as strong as ever. She wanted his love. But not only for an evening, not even for a year or two. She knew that all it would take was one word, one look and he'd be with her. It would take nothing to have him for the night. But one night wasn't good enough. She wanted his love for ever. Only for ever was good enough.

But a man like Nick needed his freedom. A man like Nick couldn't settle for a placid domestic life.

With a man like Nick, there was no for ever.

The first part of the project was drawing to a close. Megan had organised the co-operative—the people from the flood village who would buy in to the new housing project, bought from the government on easy terms. The housing design, with all the changes and adaptations, had been finalised. The two temporary consultants, John, the construction engineer and Maxie Goodwin, the cost analyst/financial planner, were due to arrive Saturday afternoon to help write up the final project presentation which included the full description, designs, site lay-out, budget, utilities and description of the co-operative for approval in Jakarta. After that, construction would begin.

'Are you coming to the airport with me to pick up Maxie and John tomorrow?' Nick asked on Friday afternoon, as they prepared to close up the office and go home. 'We can go early and do some shopping first.'

She nodded. 'OK. I do need a few things.' She put some papers in a file and closed it. 'By the way, I'll need to go to Jakarta one of these days. My passport is going to expire. I'll need a couple of days off.'

He frowned. 'Can it wait till after John and Maxie are gone?'

'Oh, sure. I've got two months or so. I just don't want to forget it.'

He thought for a moment. 'After we're finished with it, I'm going to Jakarta to deliver the final presentation to Lester

Howard. I suppose you could go, instead. Kill two birds with one stone.'

'You're the project director. Shouldn't you do it?'

He shrugged. 'I don't think it matters. Lester Howard, unfortunately, is not one of my favourite people. I'd just as soon not see him.'

'All right, then, I'll go.' Megan picked up her bag and scanned the office to see if she'd forgotten anything. 'What are you planning for Sunday for our two guests?'

He snapped his briefcase shut and strode to the door. 'We could take them to the beach and show them the tourist scene. Go out to dinner at Poppies.'

'Sounds good to me.' Poppies was one of Megan's favourite places to eat, located in a narrow alley in the beach village of Kuta. It was a garden restaurant, with an exotic junglelike setting, that served the most wonderful seafood. 'But are you sure you don't want to get started on the presentation?'

He grinned. 'Am I such a slave-driver?'

'Just checking. I know how eager you are to get this thing finished.'

'Well, I am, but there are limits to my ambition, believe it or not. Besides, they don't get paid for working on Sunday, and this is Bali, after all.' He opened the door for her. 'I'll pick you up tomorrow morning at nine.'

Waiting at airports was not one of her favourite activities. Megan looked around restlessly. The plane was half an hour late, but finally John and Maxie came through. Maxie looked great, wearing a pair of stylish white trousers and a loose flowered shirt and a bright smile to match. She hugged Nick with enthusiasm.

'How are you? Nice to see you again!'

They shook hands all around, Megan feeling her smile grow stiff on her face as she listened to Maxie's cheerful laughter.

'Look at that tan!' she said, surveying Nick with teasing eyes. 'Do you do any work at all, or do you just spend your days at the beach?'

'Unfortunately, most of my days are spent inside the gloomiest office you've ever seen,' he assured her.

'Worse than Thailand?'

He nodded. 'Worse.'

Maxie made a face. 'Then you *should* spend your days at the beach. But no, not you. Work before pleasure as always, I assume.' She turned to face Megan and John. 'You should have seen him in Thailand. I've never worked so hard in my life!'

Megan was silent most of the way home, letting the others do the talking. Maxie was sitting in the front next to Nick, and Megan was in the back with John. He was tall and lean, and in his fifties still looked like an athlete. He told her he ran twenty-five to thirty miles every week, no matter where he was.

The two of them stayed in the village, in a small tourist hotel that consisted mostly of a collection of romantic cottages with thatched roofs. There was an ice-cold swimming pool fed by a mountain stream meandering through the grounds. It was an idyllic place, if not the height of luxury and comfort, and they seemed more than happy with the arrangements.

Megan was unable to suppress a feeling of unease at the thought of Maxie Goodwin being on the island. She'd only be there for three weeks, and Megan wasn't sure why she felt the way she did.

By the end of the fourth day, she knew.

Maxie Goodwin was in love with Nick.

By the end of the seventh day, she knew something else.

She was jealous.

More jealous that she had ever been in her life. It was a horrible, ugly feeling, a sickness of the heart, a constant ache, a seething anger she couldn't control. She knew with a painful certainty that she didn't want Nick to fall in love with Maxie.

But she could hardly blame him if he did. She'd certainly not given him any reason not to, giving him no encouragement, being on friendly terms only. Her message had been clear: I don't want you.

Maxie was nice and smart and attractive in an interesting way. Megan couldn't find anything to hate her for. Nick and Maxie got on famously. They both worked like horses and made up a smooth working team. It was obvious they knew each other well, and were familiar with each other's working habits. They joked and laughed, talking about people and experiences Megan didn't know about. She felt excluded, left out, and she resented it.

Two more weeks, she reminded herself. Two more weeks and she'll be gone. Two more weeks was an eternity.

John, too, was a hard worker. Fortunately, he saw eye to eye with them on the design of the houses, making few changes and suggestions. Apart from the office, they saw little of him. He was either out running in the muggy heat, or swimming in the freezing swimming pool. The man must be in fantastic condition, Megan thought, wondering where he got the energy. He ate little and talked less.

At Nick's suggestion, they had moved the office temporarily to one of the empty rooms in his house. It was cooler there and more comfortable than in the crowded, drab government office. Ibu, Nick's cook, was available to supply them with food and drinks, without them having to go out for them. The office computer, a portable, was transferred, and the computer carried in by John and Maxie was set up as well.

They worked together, had lunch together, and spent some of their free time together, as Megan and Nick showed John and Maxie the island attractions. Megan watched Maxie and Nick, resenting their easy-going camaraderie, feeling more miserable by the day.

Sometimes she'd go home, leaving the two of them still at the computers, working out financial problems. Her imagination went wild. What would they do when they were alone? Would Maxie stay for dinner at Nick's house? Would they spend the evening together? Sleep together?

One more week, she said to herself as she walked home one evening. One more week and they'll be gone. She was tired and depressed. She didn't need all this emotional turmoil, along with the stress of finishing the presentation. She passed by the village shops, glancing unseeingly at the paintings and the carvings, absently greeting familiar faces.

'I have new sarongs! They come today. You want to see?' The young girl in the shop door looked at her with eager eyes.

Megan smiled at her and shook her head. 'Not today.' She had sarongs in every colour of the rainbow, plus a few more. Plain ones, fancy ones, silver-threaded ones. What would she do with all those sarongs once she was back in the States?

She walked up the uneven path to her house, inspecting the guava tree for ripe fruit. None today. Maybe in a couple more days. She opened the front door, then stopped as she noticed the man sitting in a chair.

'Hello, Megan.'

She stared at him, not believing her eyes. 'Sam?' she asked at last.

He grinned. 'The very one. I'm glad you remembered me this time.' He got out of the chair, stood in front of her, took her hand and shook it cordially.

CHAPTER SEVEN

'WHAT are you doing here?' Blond Sam did not belong here. He was like an apparition from another lifetime. There was a vague memory of a warm fire on a cold November night, a delicious turkey dinner, and Sam seducing her with his eyes across the pumpkin pie.

'Just checking if you've done any more repressing.' He was still holding her hand, and Megan extracted it from his grip with difficulty.

'How did you get here?' she asked stupidly. What was Sam doing here, at the other side of the world?'

He leaned his blond head a little closer, eyes sparkling with laughter. 'It's a secret,' he whispered, 'but I'll tell you, if you promise not to tell anybody. It's magic. I'm a warlock, you see. I say a secret incantation, wiggle my ears and *pfooff!* off I go, any place I like.'

She gave him a long-suffering look and dropped her briefcase on a chair. 'Right, I should have guessed.'

He looked wounded. 'I'd hoped for a more enthusiastic welcome.'

'I'm sorry, I have no enthusiasm left.' It didn't sound very nice, and she felt a twinge of guilt. She sighed, then forced a smile. 'I've had a rotten day. Maybe you have some magic for that, Mr Warlock?'

'A rotten day? We allow no rotten days on Bali.' He reached in his pocket and took out a balloon, which he proceeded to blow up as she watched in utter amazement. He twisted and turned as he blew, and somehow the amorphous piece of orange material ended up looking like a happy puppy.

From another pocket he took a felt-tipped pen, and moments late two bright eyes peered at her curiously.

He handed it over to her. 'To keep you happy and joyful.'

Megan couldn't help but smile as she took the balloon from him. 'I'm impressed,' she said as she examined the puppy. 'Pretty clever.'

'I know,' he agreed, apparently not given to humility. 'I'll make you a bunny or a cat or whatever you like, if you'll feed me dinner.'

'Thanks. One puppy is all I need, but I'll offer you dinner for free.'

'You're very generous.'

'I know,' she said, and Sam laughed.

Over an elaborate dinner of Balinese pork, served up by a smiling Ariaso, he told her he was going to start work seriously in the autumn, sharing a thriving practice with another doctor in a small but growing community. His grandfather, who had more money than he knew what to do with, had offered him a trip around the world as a present and a last fling before settling down to the serious business of being a doctor. 'How could I refuse?' he asked.

'I don't see how,' Megan agreed, taking a bite of steamed rice. 'We should all have grandfathers like him.'

He nodded his agreement. 'So, here I am. I started off in Europe. Ah, the wine, the girls . . .' he sighed. 'I was in India for a while. Fascinating. Then Thailand, Malaysia, Java, and here I am, sitting in your house, eating at your table. Amazing, isn't it? Such a coincidence.'

Megan nodded. 'Definitely a miracle.'

His eyes were laughing. 'It was an opportunity not to be missed.'

'Of course, she said drily. 'Have some more rice.'

'You don't take me seriously, do you?'

'What's there to take seriously?'

Sam gave her an injured look. 'You think I'm a light-hearted, no-god philanderer.'

She smiled sweetly. 'I think you're going to be a wonderful paediatrician.'

'You couldn't possibly accept that, ever since my sister brought you home, I've been head over heels in love with you?'

'Not a chance.' She pushed her plate away. 'Would you like some dessert? We have fresh fruit salad. Mango, star fruit, pawpaw, pineapple. Or black rice pudding.'

He made a face. 'Black rice pudding? Sounds revolting!'

Megan laughed. 'Not a very enlightened comment from a world traveller. It's very nice. You should try it.'

'All right, I will.'

'Brave man. Tell me, where are you staying?'

'Not here, I imagine.'

'Definitely not.'

Sam sighed, his face a mask of dejection. 'In that case, I'm staying in a small *losmen* at Kuta beach. Very basic, but clean and close to the beach.'

Ariaso discreetly stuck her head around the door. *'Sudah?'* she enquired.

Megan nodded. 'We're finished. We'll have some of the black rice pudding, please.' Ariaso padded in on bare feet, took away the dishes and replaced them with a bowl of rice pudding. Sam watched her disappear into the kitchen.

'You've got it made, haven't you? A house, a maid, a job, and all that on Bali.'

'Right.' She was surprised to hear the bitterness in her own voice. It didn't elude Sam, either. He have her a sharp look. 'Trouble in paradise?' he asked.

Her shrug was light. 'Let's just say it's not what I had expected.'

On Saturday, they toured the island, running into a temple ceremony in a small town, and getting caught up in the colour and excitement of the festivities. The temple was all decorated in strips of white fabric, flowers, and brightly coloured ceremonial unbrellas. People wore brilliant brocade sarongs, *gamelan* bands played music for hours on end, children laughed and danced and played.

Sam enjoyed himself tremendously, apparently much given to noise and colour and fun.

'There's a funeral in Ubud next week,' Megan told him as they drove back to Kuta, where she would drop Sam off at his *losmen*. 'Would you like me to see if I can get you a ticket?'

He stared at her. 'A ticket for a *funeral?*'

She laughed. 'Funerals are very festive occasions, and very expensive. It makes business sense to have the *turis* help with the payment.'

'You're kidding me!' he said incredulously.

'Absolutely not. Haven't you read your guide book?'

'Why is it a festive occasion, for Pete's sake? Are they glad to see their people depart?'

'I'm sure they've done their mourning. From what I hear, the old man died months ago, but the funeral is a special ceremony to liberate the soul from its earthly body. They build an enormous towerlike structure, more ornate you've never seen, put the body or remains in it and burn the whole affair to send off the soul to the spirit world. Definitely a time of celebration.'

'Sounds like something I shouldn't miss,' he said, sounding rather doubtful.

'Not if you want to say you've been to Bali.'

Sunday they spent at the beach. Megan saw him several times during the following week, usually finding him waiting at her house after she got back from work. Despite herself, she had to admit she was having fun. Sam's light-heartedness made her feel carefree and happy. He made her laugh. He took her mind off Maxie and Nick—at least for short times.

The last week came to a close, and Maxie and John flew out of Denpasar on Saturday afternoon. Megan sighed with relief.

There was a party that night, and she was looking forward to a little relaxation.

They had one more week to edit the final draft of the presentation, and a week from Monday she would handcarry it herself to the US Agency for International Development offices in Jakarta. She couldn't wait to get rid of the thing and go on with the real work: the construction of the houses themselves.

She searched through her wardrobe to find a dress to wear for the party. She took out a bright African print in green and blue and white that she'd bought in Sierra Leone. It was a long cotton dress with a wide band of intricate embroidery around the neckline and the edge of the wide sleeves. It looked rather exotic, which was all right for her state of mind tonight.

She brushed her hair till it shone, put some long, dangly earrings in her ears and looked at herself with satisfaction.

The party was held just down the road, and it took her only a few minutes to get there.

'Well, well, don't you look gorgeous!' Nick greeted her as she made her entrance. His blue eyes laughed at her as he surveyed her dress. 'The stamp of Africa. Let me guess. Difinitely West Coast. Sierra Leone, perhaps?'

'I marvel at your fashion knowledge,' she answered. 'Let me get a drink—I need one.'

'So do I.' He followed her to the bar and raised his glass to her as soon as she had her own. 'Let us toast to the successful completion of the final presentation.'

Megan let out a martyred sigh. 'Oh, please, yes. One more week. I don't know if I'll live through it. I hate paperwork, reports, financial statements.'

'So I've noticed,' Nick agreed. 'You've been in a terrible mood the last few weeks.' He drank deeply from his glass. 'Anyway, if will all be over soon, and John and Maxie are out of the way now. The more people, the longer it takes.'

'I thought you'd be sorry to see Maxie go.'

'I'm always sorry to see Maxie go,' he said blandly. 'She's a pleasure to work with, didn't you think so?'

Megan nodded. 'Yes.' It was the truth; she couldn't very well say anything else. 'She told me you worked together on a project in Thailand,' she said casually.

'We did. She was there for six months. Don't know what I would have done without her.'

Somebody started some music. 'Dance, ladies and gentlemen, dance!' Brian Williams was at it again, complete with flowered shirt and cigar.

Nick took her arm. 'I suppose we'd better obey the master.'

They began to move to the music, as did several other couples. It was a fast number that inspired some of them to go into the strangest contortions, twisting and bending and leaping, with a primitive exuberance that defied the heat.

'And now, ladies and gentlemen,' the Sultan announced with the number was finished, 'we have something for the golden oldies among us. All you old folks who can't keep up, this is for you.'

It was a slow, romantic tune that was received with a few boos, yet none of the guests sat down, and they all ended up entwined in their mate's arms. Nick smiled down at Megan seductively as he took her hand and put his other arm around her back.

'Now this is what I call dancing,' he whispered in her ear as he moulded her against him.

Her every nerve-ending was aware of Nick's body against hers, and she tensed, resisting the pressure of his hand on her back, trying to keep some space between them.

'Relax,' he whispered. 'It's more fun that way.'

Too bad Maxie is gone, she was tempted to say. She'd love it if you'd hold her like this. But she had more sense than to voice the thought. She wasn't giving Nick more ammunition to use against her.

'Where's the blond beach boy on the motor-cycle?' he

asked, his mouth close to her ear. 'Isn't he here with you?'

'No.' Sam had gone to a Monkey Dance at the village square.

'Who is he? A new beau?'

'Someone I know from home,' she answered stiffly, feeling her hackles rise.

'Ah, an old beau.'

'Oh, shut up!'

Nick laughed softly. 'What's he doing on Bali?'

'Why all the interest?'

He shrugged lightly. 'Just making conversation.'

'I see. Well, Sam's here to see me. He's on a trip around the world, and by accident ended up on Bali. You know how it goes.'

She could feel him tense fractionally. His arm tightened slightly, drawing her face against his shoulder. Megan closed her eyes, trying to relax. Nick didn't like her going out with Sam. Like he hadn't liked her going out with Peter. Not that he'd ever admit it, not in a thousand years.

His conceit was unbelievable!

He still wanted her; he'd said so himself. Yet he wanted his freedom, too. He wanted to fool around with Maxie Goodwin, and have *her*, too. He didn't like it when she went out with other men. Well, he couldn't have her. There was a price to pay for his freedom and lack of commitment.

'He's not really your type, is he?' he enquired conversationally.

'Not my type? Oh, I wouldn't say so,' she said lightly, trying hard not to show her irritation. 'Sam is a lot of fun. We've been to the beach, we've been all over the island, and with him there's always a laugh.'

'He's a beach bum if I ever saw one,' he said pleasantly. 'Not what I expected of you. I thought you could do better than that.'

'I don't need to do better than that!' Her voice rose

fractionally, and she could feel her control slip.

'Oh, lighten up, Meggie. I'm merely commenting on the fact that he doesn't seem to be your type.'

Lighten up, Meggie. She hated his condescension, his arrogance. Who did he think he was?

'And who's my type?' she asked coldly. 'You? Well, let me tell you something, Mr Perfect. Sam is OK. He's a doctor, a paediatrician. He's going back home to start his practice and he'll be good! Beach bum, you say! Hah!' She took a ragged breath. 'And let me tell you something else! I like Sam! I'm having fun. What the hell is wrong with that?'

He gave her a wide-eyed, innocent look. 'Nothing! Nothing at all. By all means, have some fun!'

'Sam is special!' she continued, fired on by a sudden perverse longing to hurt him. 'He makes me laugh. He makes the children laugh. You know what he does! He has a pocket full of balloons and he blows them up for the village children and makes all kinds of animals out of them—dogs and cats and giraffes and rabbits and . . .' She rambled on.

'A wonderful man, no doubt.' said Nick drily. 'A credit to society.' The mockery was ill-concealed.

Megan clamped her jaws shut, determined not to say another word, willing the dance to end. When finally the music stopped, she walked away quickly before she would disgrace herself and hit him.

Someone touched her arm. 'Fighting with the boss?' Pam looked at her, eyes laughing. She wore loose black trousers and a red embroidered shirt, clothes that were peddled at the beach to the tourists. She looked great, despite the cheap clothes.

'I need a drink,' Megan said. 'I need a vacation. I need to get off this island.'

Pam laughed. 'Sounds like a contradiction. Don't you know people *come* here for a vacation? What's the trouble? Maxie Goodwin?'

Megan looked at her sharply. 'What do you know

about Maxie?'

Pam shrugged. 'Nothing. I just observed her a couple of times. Seems on very . . . let's say, *comfortable* terms with Nick.'

Megan grimaced. 'Regular pals, those two. They've known each other a long time. You want a drink?' She turned towards the bar and Pam followed her. Keith was in a creative mood again, and served them another one of his potions with a flourish.

'Bali Thunder,' he announced, handing them their glasses, duly decorated with frangipani blossoms and a piece of fresh pineapple.

'It had better be good,' Pam threatened. 'Last time you fixed me something, I looked green for two days!'

'Impossible,' he denied with a confident grin. 'Must have been the food.'

Megan took a careful sip. 'Not bad. I wonder what's in it.'

'Don't ask. Say, who's Mr Handsome on the motor-cycle?'

'Someone I know from back home. The brother of a friend of mine, on a tour around the world.'

'Sounds like fun. I've always wanted to do that, but I'm too chicken. I need the safety of a company to pay my way and bail me out in case of trouble. So, I take the world one piece at a time.'

'I don't think you're suffering too much.'

'I'm not complaining.' She took a courageous swallow of her drink. 'You're right. Not bad at all.'

The drink made Megan feel better, so she had another one. The music started again and she made the rounds, dancing with Peter, who was *sans femme* for the evening, with Tony, and a couple of others.

She was sitting at the bar, having another drink, when another slow, romantic tune began to waft its soft notes through the room. Nick appeared at her side and took her arm.

'Let's have another swirl,' he suggested.

'No, thanks. I'm done dancing.'

'Done drinking too, I hope.'

The heat of fury rushed through her. 'What the . . .'

He swung her off her stool and into his arms with a single pull of his hand. 'I've been watching you. You're overdoing it a bit, sweetheart. One more and you're going to make a fool of yourself.'

'If I want to make a fool of myself, that's my business!'

'Mine, too,' said Nick calmly. 'I'm the boss, remember?'

Megan gritted her teeth and didn't answer. Her head was too fuzzy for fighting.

Again he held her very close, and for a while they danced without speaking. The music was soothing. In spite of herself, Megan could feel herself begin to relax. She closed her eyes. The drink had mellowed her. She fitted so comfortably against him—they moved so easily to the music. If only she could forget it was Nick holding her, she could enjoy it. But she was enjoying it . . . in a way she didn't really want to. It was too sensual, too exciting, to feel his body move against hers, to feel the warmth of it through her clothes.

'I like dancing with you,' he said after a pause. 'I always liked dancing with you. Do you remember that night I came back, after I'd been gone six weeks to . . .'

She felt a spasm of pain. 'Don't,' she said huskily. 'Please, don't.' She closed her eyes, as if it would help block out the memory, but it was there, called up by his words, and there was no pushing it back.

She saw again the bedroom, replete with flowers and candles, a bottle of champagne on the dresser. She heard the soft music drifting in from the stereo in the living-room. And Nick was holding her like this, arms around her, dancing to the music.

'I've missed you,' he whispered in her ear, his hand sliding under her blouse and stroking her bare back.

'I missed you, too,' she whispered back. 'The bed is too

big without you. I hate waking up alone.'

He kissed her eyes, her cheeks, her mouth, his hand moving to her front and slowly unbuttoning her blouse. He began to undress her, kissing and dancing at the same time, one piece of clothing at a time. She did the same to him. It took a long time, a long, delicious, tantalising time, and finally they were dancing in the nude, holding each other, kissing and touching, until desire made her knees weak. He laid her down on the bed, and all the slow gentleness vanished; there was nothing but impatience and the mutual rapturous passion too long restrained. Six weeks had passed, and she knew with unshaking certainty that she would alway love him, no matter how long he'd be gone.

All that had been a long time ago and Megan didn't want him to remind her now. She didn't want to remember the love she had once felt for him.

He held her away from him a little and looked at her, his eyes laughing. 'But I like to remember that night,' he said, as if he could read her feelings. His mouth quirked into a smile. 'It was very special. I'd never before danced with a naked woman in my arms.'

She didn't know why, but something snapped inside her. Maybe it was the drink. Maybe it was the tension that had built inside her over the past three weeks, watching him carry on with Maxie.

'Bastard!' she whispered fiercely. 'How dare you do . . . do this to me? How . . .' Her voice broke. Tears spilled from her eyes. She tried to break loose from his grip, but he held her tight, his arms like a vice. 'Let go of me!' Her voice rose to a loud pitch. She didn't care that everybody in the room could hear her. She didn't care about anything but trying to get away from him.

Nick held on to her as he led her out the open doors to the garden, which lay quiet and serene, bathing in silver moonlight.

'Let me go!' she cried, tears running down her cheeks. 'I hate you! I hate what you're doing to me!'

'What am I doing to you?'

'You know what you're doing! You're always bringing up memories! Things from . . . from before.' She swallowed hard. 'It hurts! Don't you understand? It hurts to remember those things. It hurts to think of the time when I loved you, when I thought you loved me. You're doing this deliberately, and I don't know why! You could be a little more sensitive to my feelings!'

'How sensitive are you to mine?'

'I hadn't noticed you had any!'

'Maybe you should pay a little more attention.'

'All you want is to sleep with me! Maxie's barely gone and here you are, back again!'

There was a short, heavy silence. 'Maxie has nothing to do with this. She's a friend—a good friend, but nothing more.'

'Friend, my foot! She's head over heels in love with you and don't deny it! Not that I care! You can have all the women you want, but not me!'

'I don't want other women. I don't want Maxie. I want you.'

'Well, you can't have me!' Megan swung away from him, making for the door, but he grabbed her and hauled her against him, crushing her mouth with his. He kissed her until she was nothing but a quivering mass of nerves and tremulous desire.

Then, with the last remnants of her strength, she tore away from him. 'You . . .' she began.

'I am *not* in love with Maxie,' Nick interrupted her, his voice hard and determined. 'And I never was.'

'Well, she . . .'

'Hey! Donovan!' a voice called out into the night. 'No necking in the dark! There's somebody here to see you!'

He gave her one last, burning look, then stalked off towards the house.

She wasn't going back inside. She walked out the back gate, her legs unsteady, her face still flushed with his heated kisses. The road was dark, but she had walked it many times. Most people had long gone to bed. Just before she reached her gate, she heard the footsteps.

'Megan!'

She didn't answer, but closed the gate behind her and walked up to the house.

The gate creaked. Fury overwhelmed her. 'Go away!'

'I want to talk to you.'

'I've got nothing to say!'

He was next to her, taking her arm, and she wrenched herself free. 'Don't you touch me!'

Then she saw the motor-cycle leaning against the house, and in the glow of the outside light she noticed Sam's dark shape propped up against his duffel-bag in front of the door.

'Well, well,' came Nick's voice, slow and icy cold. 'You've got company. Did he lose the key? Well, don't let me hold you up.' He turned on his heel and marched off, slamming the gate.

Sam came slowly to his feet, raking a sleepy hand through his hair.

'I must have fallen asleep,' he said dazedly. He looked like a little boy, lost and confused. 'I was waiting for you. There was nobody here.'

'It's after twelve, Sam. What are you doing here?'

He pushed his hands into the pockets of his shorts and hunched his shoulders slightly. 'You're not going to believe it, but I was robbed on the beach this afternoon. All my money is gone. My traveller's cheques, everything.'

'Good lord, how did that happen? You'd better come inside.' Megan took her key and opened the door.

She made him a drink and Sam told her the story. It wasn't much of a story at all, just that he had fallen asleep on the beach and someone had taken his wallet out of his shorts' pocket.

'You had *all* your money with you?'

I figured it was safer on me than alone in my room.'

'What about your passport?'

'I've still got that.'

Megan let out a slow sigh. 'Thank God! That would be a major hassle.' She frowned. 'I suppose, without money, you have no place to sleep. You'd better stay here until you've got it sorted out.'

Sam grinned gratefully. 'I'd hoped you'd say that. I promise I'll try to get out of here as soon as I can. I'll have to get my bank to wire me some more money. I'll see if I can get those traveller's cheques replaced. I can't do anything till Monday, though.'

'It's all right.' She rubbed her forehead. She had a splitting headache. 'I'll get you some sheets and towels. You can sleep in the room at the end of the hall, second on the left.'

'Thanks.'

It took him several days to sort it out, but on Wednesday evening, at dinner, he triumphantly waved a wad of rupiah notes in front of her face and announced that he was leaving the next morning. If she didn't mind, he added, he'd like to stay here just one more night so he could go see the *Wayang Kulit* shadow play, in a neighbouring village, that would run through most of the night. 'You want to come with me to see it?' he asked hopefully. 'Maybe you can explain it to me.'

She laughed. 'No way. I haven't a clue.' The one time she'd seen the ancient play, she'd been lost in the symbolism and spiritualism, and bewildered by the endless parade of different characters portrayed by leather puppets—demons and deities, kings and queens, and even several clowns—telling a story of good and evil. Her Indonesian had not been up the complexities of the tale, and the mystical and religious connotations had eluded her.

'Besides,' she went on, 'I can't afford to be up half

the night.' She was exhausted. Her head and eyes ached after
spending the last few days peering at the computer screen,
editing the report. Nick was at his worst, snapping at her,
criticising her writing, her spelling, her style. Then for hours
he would ignore her, and go off into a morose silence and read
and re-read the report, only to come back with   more
corrections and alterations. For some reason, the work was not
going well. It was taking too much time. If the pace didn't pick
up soon, they wouldn't get it done before Monday, whether
they worked through the weekend or not.

Nick's frame of mind was not positively influenced, either,
by the fact that the Toyota had been damaged in an accident.
On Saturday night, Atjin, the driver, a handsome young Don
Juan Bali-style, had taken the car without authorisation, driven
it into Denpasar for a night on the town with his girlfriend,
and crashed it into a wall. It was the news Nick had received
the night of the party. Fortunately, neither Atjin nor his
girlfriend had been injured.

Having warned Atjin twice before about the unauthorised
use of a government vehicle, Nick had fired him on the spot,
leaving them with no one to carry messages, to pick up and
deliver mail or to run errands in general. It was a most
inopportune time for a complication of this sort. All Megan
could think of was to get the week over with, to ship off the
presentation to Jakarta, and take a few days off to relax. And
right now what she wanted was a long night's
sleep—preferably free of puppets and music and mysticism.

After dinner, Sam took off on his motor-cycle to see his
Wayang Kulit play, and Megan took a long, relaxing shower,
washed her hair and polished her nails. She would have liked
to read, but her eyes refused to function.

There was a knock on the door as she finished the last coat of
nail polish and, waving her hands to dry the lacquer, she
opened the door.

'I want to talk to you.'

Nick. Mouth grim, eyes a little wild, hair falling over his forehead. He stepped past her into the room. 'Where is he?'

'Who?' She tensed in anger.

'That beach boy! Sam What's-his-name.'

'I don't see that it's any of your business,' she said icily.

'I'm making it my business!'

'Oh?'

His eyes were blue steel. 'I want him to leave,' he said with cold determination. 'I want him out of your house. I want him to get his act together and sashay on with his goddamned tour around the world.'

She stared at him, then gave a short, humourless laugh. 'You've got to be kidding!'

'I'm not kidding.' There was a murderous look in his eyes.

'This is *my* house.'

'And I don't want him in it.'

There was a silence as she digested this. 'You sound jealous,' she said at last.

Nick looked at her squarely. 'I *am* jealous.'

She gaped at him. 'What is this? A joke?'

'No, goddamn it!'

She was stunned by this uncharacteristic confession. Nick was jealous. He really way. She could see the truth of it in his eyes, the expression on his face, the rigid stance of his body.

'It's not a pretty emotion,' he said huskily. 'It's irrational. It's primitive. It's territorial. It's destructive. All right, I know all that. I've fought it, but I can't seem to do a damned thing about it. It makes my insides hurt. I want that freeloader out of your house, or I won't be responsible for my actions.'

Megan could tell him it was none of his business whom she had in her house. None of his business whom she spent her time with. He had no right to demand that she throw Sam out. No right at all! Yet his blunt confession had melted away all her outrage and indignation.

'He's leaving tomorrow,' she said.

'Thank you.' Nick held her eyes for a moment, then turned and strode out into the night.

She stared after him. She could not believe what had just happened, or what it meant.

The next few days they worked on the report till eight or nine at night. They were still in Nick's house and Megan ate her meals with him, cooked by a worried Ibu. She kept shaking her head at them, telling them they worked too hard, *terlalu keras*, and would make themselves *sakit* if they didn't slow down. She concocted wonderful dishes and exotic snacks to sustain them through the day.

Nick did not mention Sam, who had departed on Thursday morning, but the atmosphere was still tense, if not as explosive as it had been in the beginning of the week.

They worked all day Saturday but, by nine at night, they were still not finished.

'We'll have to do the rest tomorrow,' Nick said, throwing down his pen.

'I don't want to,' Megan said, peering at the screen and inserting another line of Nick's inimitable prose. 'I'd rather just stay here now and work till it's done. Give me a cup of coffee and a ten-minute break and I'll do it.'

'I can't ask that of you.'

'You're not asking—I'm offering. I don't want to give up my Sunday, for one thing. I'm going strong now. Let's just keep going.' She gave the computer the command to save, and leaned back in her chair. 'Right, that's section seven. The next one is pretty good as it stands, I think. Have you gone through it yet?'

For the next few hours they worked in smooth, efficient co-operation, in spite of their fatigue. Four hours and four cups of coffee later, the report was finished.

'We did it!' Megan's voice was triumphant. She gave the computer the command to print. A moment later paper started rolling out of the printer and the rattling noise that filled the room sounded like music. She gave a deep sigh and leaned back in her chair, smiling up at Nick. He looked tired but relieved, and he grinned back at her.

'I'll get us a long, cool drink.'

'Good, I can use one.' She looked down at her wrinkled dress and made a face. She felt sticky and hot and tired. 'And I can use a long, cool shower, too. After which I intend to sleep until noon tomorrow.'

Some time later she gathered up the printed report, tore off the perforated strips and separated the pages.

'Doesn't this look wonderful?' She felt almost euphoric with relief. The damned thing was finished. Now the real job could begin—building houses for people to live in.

Nick nodded his agreement, taking in a thirsty swallow from his glass. 'Best piece of writing in all the East.'

She handed him the stack of paper with a little bow. 'Here you go, sir. Go sock it to them!'

He gave a crooked smile. 'You're the one who's going to deliver it.'

'Right, I forgot.' She took a long drink from her gin and tonic, almost finishing it in one go. 'I didn't know I was so thirsty,' she said, smiling.

'There's plenty more.' He put the paper on the table. 'Thank's for sticking with me.'

She waved if off carelessly. 'It was nothing.'

'It's one o'clock in the morning. I couldn't have done it without you.'

They smiled at each other, and suddenly the smile faded from Megan's face. There was a dark glow in his eyes, a look she recognised. Her heart began to hammer nervously.

'It's very late,' he said softly.

'Yes.' Why didn't she move? Why was she standing there, staring into his eyes like a fool?

He reached out and took her hands. 'Megan?'

Her throat went dry and the silence seemed to echo in the room. She wanted to say something, crack a joke, laugh, anything to break the tension that surrounded them. But there was nothing, only his eyes and the silence and the memories they shared of happier times in other places.

His hands reached up and touched her hair, smoothing it. She didn't move. Her arms hung by her sides, as if she were a rag doll without a will of her own. She closed her eyes, fighting emotions and desires that threatened to overwhelm her.

It was insanity to stand here and let him touch her! Insanity that she was incapable of moving, of speaking. She was aware of it, yet felt powerless against the force of what was happening.

His hands stroked her eyelids, her cheeks. His thumb gently traced the contours of her mouth. Her hands clenched into fists by her sides and her knees felt weak. Then she felt his mouth on hers—not a kiss, really, but a featherlike caress that sent her senses soaring. She wanted to hold him, wanted to kiss him and touch him and make love. Still she could not make herself respond, her mouth did not answer his kiss, her arms would not move to embrace him.

'Megan?' he whispered against her mouth.

She opened her eyes, meeting his.

He moved away slightly, holding her gaze. 'Please, Megan, stay with me tonight.'

The room was silent again. She heard the blood pounding in her ears. A deep, painful hunger ached inside her. She moistened her lips, feeling reason recede. There was no past, no future. There was only now and the man she loved.

'All right,' she whispered.

CHAPTER EIGHT

THE room was cool and washed in the silvery light of the full moon. A breeze wafted in through the open windows, touching Megan's heated skin, carrying with it the lonely cry of some nocturnal bird and the babble of the creek at the bottom of the garden.

'Sit down,' said Nick softly, handing Megan one of the glasses of wine he'd carried in. He did not turn on the light, but took her hand and led her to the bed, drawing her down next to him.

'To us,' he said, raising the glass, then drinking from it. The wine was fruity, but not too sweet, and she sipped it slowly while Nick's hand played with her fingers, stroking and caressing with seemingly innocent intimacy.

'You have no curtains in here,' she said.

He gave a crooked smile. 'No. Does that bother you?'

'I guess not. There's nothing out there.'

'Nothing but the night. It makes me feel like I'm sleeping outside. I can see the stars and the palms, and I can hear the water and the wind, and in the morning the birds wake me up.' He took the empty glass from her fingers and put it on the table.

'You sound so romantic,' she said, hearing the smile in her voice.

'Maybe I am.' Wine-cooled lips found hers. His arms moved around her and locked her against him. 'I've dreamed of making love to you again,' he whispered against her mouth, 'of holding you in my arms, here in this bed.'

Warmth spread through her, mingling with the heady feel

153

of the wine in her blood. She moved her lips against his in answer, and he let out a soft groan as his kiss changed into a deep, urgent exploration. Megan laced her fingers through the thick dark hair, revelling in the feel of it against her skin, the feel of his mouth on hers.

Nick drew back a little, his hands coming forward, stroking her breasts through the thin material of her dress. Flames leaped inside her and her breath came out in shallow puffs of air.

'You still want that long, cool shower?' he whispered.

She shook her head. 'A short, warm one.'

He laughed softly. 'How about a long, hot one, with me?' He began to unbutton her dress, not waiting for an answer, sliding if off her shoulders. 'Stand up.'

They undressed each other with urgent, trembling hands, eager mouths kissing exposed skin. His body gleamed in the pale light, long and sleek, and she slid her hands over the hair-roughened chest, feeling the strong beat of his heart under her palms.

How they managed to make it from the bedroom into the shower, Megan didn't know. Everything seemed unreal, and the hot stream of water did nothing to cool her down. She was conscious only of the two of them, the utter sensitivity of her own senses, and the virile masculinity of Nick's naked body, so familiar, yet still so overwhelmingly exciting.

He curved his hands around her breasts, slightly lifting them so their weight rested on his palms. 'You're beautiful,' he said, caressing and kissing every inch of her body, arousing her to dizzy heights of pleasure. She clung to him giddily and he moved against her, slippery with soap, until she went weak with desire and her legs would no longer support her.

Moments later they were back on the bed, warm and still slightly damp, and he cradled her against the length of his body, lying very still.

'I want this to last,' he said softly. 'Don't move or

I'll explode.'

She moaned in protest. 'You're cruel. How long?'

'At least another two minutes.'

She laughed softly. 'It's a deal.'

Through the open windows she could see a dark sky full of stars and a glorious silver moon, radiating pale light on to the bed.

'Full moon,' Nick murmured, his gaze following hers. 'I ordered it specially.' His hand began to stroke her body with slow, velvety caresses.

The whispering of the palm fronds outside the window and the soft rushing of water were mesmerising sounds in the dark, heightening her awareness of her body's responses, somehow becoming part of them, part of the tender feelings of love, awakening her deepest yearnings like a spell of the senses. Warmth and delight shivered through her. She felt like a bird, soaring high and free of earthly ties, sensing nothing but the wind and the clouds and the sun warming her body.

But it was not the sun warming her now, not the sun heating her blood and making it rush like liquid fire through her body, but Nick's hands, knowledgeable and gentle, his face tender and loving. She drowned in the shadowy blue pools of his eyes as he leaned over her, gazing down at her.

She cradled his face between her hands, drawing it close to her, and a sigh escaped him, feathering across her cheeks. His mouth moved against hers and her lips parted. His tongue touched hers with warm, moist intimacy. The familiar taste of him intoxicated her and she closed her eyes, feeling waves of sweet desire wash over her with increasing strength.

She marvelled at his restraint. She wondered how long he could keep this up, this tantalising torture of tender, teasing touches that had her teetering on the brink of insanity. He was a master—a master of touch, a master of control. But eventually desire broke down his restraint and passion consumed him until his body pressed her against him with sudden wild abandon. He moaned into her mouth and his body shook as they melded together.

No longer was there the soft whispering of the breeze, but a warm, stormy summer wind, sweeping her along, high up into the turbulence of swirling water, rushing, rushing—a glittering waterfall, cascading into unknown depths, sparking silvery splashes of light and fire.

Then all was quiet again, but for the peaceful babble of the creek and the gentle rustling of the palms as she lay quivering breathlessly in Nick's arms.

He held her lightly against him, her head cradled against his neck. They were both silent, and after a while she slowly drifted back to earth. She could feel his arms relax around her as he began to doze off. She moved away and looked at the dark face next to her on the pillow, bathed in the pale moonlight.

He opened his eyes and his hand reached out to her. 'Stay close to me.'

Megan wanted to put her arms around him, tell him she loved him, tell him she never wanted to let him go, but something stopped her, some thread of fear, an echo of the past—words he had spoken so long ago . . . 'You love me too much. You smother me . . .'

Her warm, peaceful contentment froze, and cold misery began to shiver through her. Was this what she had yearned for these past, endless months? Nick's arms around her again, Nick making love to her again? But a night of passion, no matter how perfect, was still only that—momentary rapture that had no lasting value.

What had happened to her resolve to want nothing less than for ever? Was it going to start all over again?

'What is it?' he whispered, turning on his side and touching her cheek.

Megan looked away. 'Nothing.'

'It was good, wasn't it?'

She nodded, her throat suddenly thick with tears. She rolled away from him, got out of bed and rushed into the bathroom.

She locked the door, a sob breaking loose. She didn't want him to hear her, so she turned on the shower, then sat down on a small rattan stool and wept, covering her face with her hands.

She didn't know she had so many tears to shed. Her body ached, her eyes burned. She didn't know how long she sat there, hunched over on the stool, grief and fear pouring out of her every pore. Coming to Bali had been a terrible mistake. She would never get Nick out of her system. He was part of her, yet he was not wholly hers.

Her tears spent, she took a deep, shuddering breath, then slowly got up and got under the shower, shivering with the sudden cold. She gritted her teeth, not turning on the hot water to warm it, and after a few minutes she felt calmness return.

She took a towel off the bar, still damp from their shower earlier. She held it to her face and took a deep breath.

I'll be OK, she thought. I'll be OK.

She came back into the bedroom, grateful for the darkness, so Nick couldn't see her face. Despite the cold shower, she was sure it bore traces of her crying.

'That was a long shower,' he said, reaching out his arm to her. 'Come here.'

'No, I'd better go now.' She picked up her clothes from the floor.

There was a moment of silence. 'I don't want you to go, Megan. I want you to stay with me, here, in my bed.'

'I'd better get some sleep,' she said lightly. 'A couple of hours, anyway.'

He sat up and switched on the bedside lamp. 'Megan, what's the matter?'

She turned away from him as she put on her bra and panties.

'Nothing. I don't want to overstay my welcome,' she said breezily. 'You know how it is with some women. You ask them to stay the night, and the next thing you know they're fixing you breakfast. then they're leaving a few clothes, and before you know it they've moved in. Well, don't worry. I'm not one of them.'

'I'm not worried.'

'Well, just in case.' She slipped the dress over her head. 'Anyway, I'm getting up early. Pam and I are going to the fish market.' It was the first thing that entered her head. 'We want to take some pictures,' she elaborated, talking almost frantically, covering up her inner unease with words, light-hearted, meaningless words. 'And we have to be there early. You know how . . .'

'Oh, for God's sake, stop it!' The bed creaked and then Nick's arms came around her, turning her to face him. He looked at her closely. 'Have you been crying?'

'No!'

'You're lying. Now, tell me why you don't want to stay with me. And no fish stories, please.'

Megan looked right at him. 'I just prefer to go home now, Nick.'

'Why?'

She swallowed hard. 'Because it doesn't feel right to stay here with you.' Because I can't give you everything of myself. I've given you this and it's too much already. I can't give you more, because eventually you'll not want it.

'It doesn't *feel right*?'

Megan shook her head slowly. 'No.'

His arms fell away from her and his eyes were suddenly bleak. 'I see.' He searched her face. 'I thought it was pretty special.'

Her heart turned over in her chest, but she didn't avert her eyes. 'It was.'

'I don't understand you.'

She have a half-smile. 'I'm not sure I understand myself, either. Well, maybe I do.' She dropped a quick kiss on his cheek, and left him staring after her as she walked out of the room.

The small plane looked old and tired. The seats were narrow and the upholstery worn and less than clean. Megan settled in her chair and hoped the machine would make it off the ground. 'Workhorses of this sort,' Nick had said once, 'will make it into the next century, don't worry about it.' She decided not to.

She stashed her briefcase with the precious report safely under her seat, took a book from her bag and settled down to read.

She'd not seen Nick since she'd left his house in the early morning hours on Sunday. She'd gone home, slept till noon, then had spent the rest of the day at the beach with Pam, Tony and a couple of other friends. She'd wondered if Nick had tried to see her, but she'd come home late, after going out to dinner, and she had no way of knowing.

After they were airborne, a smiling hostess offered a small cardboard box and a cup of sweetened tea. Megan took the box, then asked for a cup of unsugared tea, and the girl went back to get it for her. Megan examined the contents of the box, discovering a piece of pink rice cake, something wrapped in a banana leaf and a small piece of chocolate. She consumed the lot and drank the tea.

Jakarta was hot and steamy. For some reason, it seemed worse than Bali—maybe because of the buildings and the traffic and the pollution. She felt hot and sticky as the taxi deposited her at the gates of the Embassy compound, where a skinny, baby-faced marine looked her over suspiciously. A security officer inside a glass cage, which was complete with short-circuit TV and no doubt a gun under the desk, presented her with a pass after he had scrutinised her identification and had satisfied himself she was a law-abiding, peaceful American citizen on legitimate business. Still, she was not allowed to wander the hallowed halls alone, and a phone call was made to Lester Howard, the AID man she was to meet. Five minutes later, a dour older woman with curly bleached hair appeared at the cage to escort her to the man's office.

Her business took no more than a few minutes. Handing over the report, making a few polite noises, was all it took, and the man behind the desk showed a depressing lack of interest. Megan wondered if he, or anybody, would ever actually read the words they had sweated over for the last few weeks.

She was ready to go when she heard a knock. A man, stocky and muscular, stood in the open doorway, one brown arm propped against the doorframe.

'Les? Sorry to interrupt. Got a telex from Washington. Stanley's on his way out.'

Megan felt a jolt of pleasant surprise as she recognised the man, the friendly brown eyes, the bushy, greying hair. Tom Marsden! What was Tom doing here in Jakarta? Then his eyes met hers and a smile spread across his face.

'Megan!' He advanced into the room.

She smiled. 'Tom! It's so nice to see you?'

He took her hand in a firm clasp. 'How are you?'

'Just fine. And you?'

'Couldn't be better.' He glanced at his watch. 'How about some lunch? You have time?'

'I'd like that. I'm finished here.'

He turned to Lester Howard. 'I'll take her off your hands, if you don't mind. I'll see you tomorrow.'

The snack bar was true-blue American. Bottles of mustard and ketchup graced the formica tables. The smell of french fries hung in the air. The menu offered hamburgers, hotdogs, a variety of sandwiches and salads. Just about everybody in the place looked American. It was almost weird to be placed so suddenly in an environment that gave no indication whatsoever that, in actual fact, this was tropical Indonesia, land of short, dark people, rice paddies and spicy food.

'Well,' she said, putting her elbows on the table and resting her chin on her hands, 'what brings you to Jakarta? Last I heard, you took a job with the World Bank.'

'So I did. I'm here on a short-term job—checking out our activities with the Ministry of Social and Human Affairs. And what are you doing in these parts?'

'I'm only in Jakarta for two days. I just delivered a paper. I'm working on the CCD housing project on Bali. I thought for a while you were going to be my boss.'

Tom raised his brows in surprise. 'How's that?'

'Don't you remember? You were considering the position of project director. Nick Donovan proposed you.'

'Nick Donovan?' He looked so confused that Megan began to feel a stirring of suspicion.

'He told me he talked to you about the job.'

He nodded slowly. 'I remember talking about the project. He never asked me to consider the job.'

'Oh.' With some effort, Megan managed a casual smile. 'I suppose I misunderstood. Well, never mind.' She looked down at the menu, pretending to study it. Nick had lied to her. Why did it not really surprise her?

'So who is the project director now?' Tom asked after they'd ordered their food.

'Nick Donovan himself,' she said, watching Tom, curious to see his reaction.

She was not disappointed. Surprise radiated from him. '*Nick?* Now why would he do that?'

'I've asked him that myself.'

Tom tapped his fingers on the table and frowned. 'He had an offer from the World Bank himself. Same time I did.' He smiled ruefully. 'A better offer than mine, to tell the truth.'

She stared at him. 'I didn't know. He never told me.' Good lord, what else was there she didn't know about? It didn't make sense. Or maybe it did. Suspicion grew as she tried to sort out this information.

There was a short pause. 'This is very interesting,' Tom said at last. 'I wonder why a man of his reputation and experience would turn down the World Bank and take on that job on Bali.'

'He wanted a change. That's what he told me.'

Tom laughed out loud. 'If you believe that, you believe anything!'

The drinks arrived. Forks, knives and spoons were placed in front of them. It gave her a moment to think. Amid the confusion in her mind, memories came back to her—things Nick had said, the way he had looked. Little things, seemingly insignificant, took on other meanings.

Tom took a long, thirsty drink from his beer. 'Nick designed the project himself, didn't he?'

She nodded. Too good to be true. The words leaped into her mind. 'Anybody else for my position?' she'd asked. No, you're it.

The waiter returned with their sandwiches, placing their plates in front of them.

'He must have had some ulterior motive,' Tom remarked, spreading mustard on his ham and cheese.

Megan stared at the food on her plate. *Ulterior motive,* she thought. *And I know what it is.*

Me!

It was Nick who picked her up at the airport the next evening. She'd spent the morning getting a new passport, and had managed an hour of shopping before getting on the plane.

'How was the big city?' he asked as they walked out to the car park to get the car.

'A big city. Hot, crowded. Give me Bali any time.'

'Did you get your passport sorted out?'

'All done. And I did the big job: handed Lester Howard the report. I don't like that guy. I came all the way from Bali, and he didn't want to give me the time of day.'

'I know. I've had a couple of run ins with the man. He has a few problems.' He unlocked the door for her and she hopped into the seat.

As they drove through the dark countryside Megan wondered if she should tell him about meeting Tom Marsden. She wanted to hear his explanation, even if she knew already what it was.

'I came to see you on Sunday night,' he said as they drove up to her house.

'I wasn't home—I went to the beach in the afternoon. Later, we all went out to eat. I didn't get back until ten.'

'I know you're tired, but could I come in and talk?'

It was a request, not an order. Nick didn't even switch off the engine, just looked at her for an answer, as if he meant to go by it. It seemed strange to see him so . . . almost subdued. She thought of all the times he'd barged in when she hadn't wanted to see him.

She nodded. 'All right. There's something I wanted to talk to you about, too.'

She went into the kitchen and poured them each a drink. 'Guess who I met in Jakarta yesterday?' she asked as she handed him the glass. 'Tom Marsden. He's in Jakarta on a short-term job. We had lunch at the Embassy snack bar.' She sat down in a chair across from him, tucking her legs underneath her.

'How is he?' asked Nick.

'Just fine. Seems to like his job.'

There was a slight pause as Nick surveyed her face. 'I imagine he told you I never offered him the job of project director.'

'Yes. But you told me you did.'

He shook his head and smiled faintly. 'No. I only made you think I did.'

'So what's the difference?'

'Only a technical one. I didn't, in actual fact, lie to you.'

'You should have been a politician,' she said mildly. She took a sip from her drink. 'Tom told me something else. He said you'd turned down a job offer from the World Bank. Apparently, a very good one.'

'So I did.'

'To do this little project on Bali?'

Nick's eyes held hers. 'No. To be with you. To try and get you back.'

The words hung in the silence. Megan felt her throat close up. He had siad it. Without joking, without making fun of it. *To be with you. To try and get you back.*

'You couldn't have done that in Washington?'

'We were never there at the same time.'

'True.' She thought of how it all had started. 'You know,' she said, her voice unsteady, 'when I first read the project description, I though it was too good to be true. The job was perfect for me. As if it had been designed especially for me.'

His mouth tilted. 'It was.'

'But how . . .'

'I kept track of you. I knew about your career, where you were, what you were doing. Then I started scouting around to see if I couldn't come up with something we could do together.'

She shook her head in bewilderment. She was stunned to find out to what lengths he had gone. She'd never heard of anyone designing such an elaborate scheme. 'And you didn't want me to know about it, because you didn't think I'd accept the job if I knew.'

His blue gaze held hers. 'Would you have?'

She gave a half-smile. 'No.'

Nick swirled the ice-cubes in his glass. 'I wanted you back, Megan,' he said quietly. 'That's what this was all about. I wanted time with you. I wanted another chance. I wanted you to fall in love with me again. Sometimes I was convinced you still loved me, and then . . .' He shrugged, the words trailing away.

Tears rushed into her eyes. 'Oh, Nick . . . sometimes I don't know what it is I feel for you any more—whether it's love, or the longing for a memory, or just . . . physical need.'

'Maybe it's all three.'

Maybe it was. She'd fought her feelings because she didn't trust him any more, because she didn't want to be rejected again. But knowing what he had done for her made everything seem different. But there were still the doubts and fears, and the memories of his words.

'You weren't happy with me before,' she said, her voice low. 'If it didn't work then, why would it now?'

'It's two years later. We're both older and wiser. I've learned a few truths in the past few years.'

'And what are those?'

'Love is not something to take for granted, for one.' Nick stood up and came towards her, reaching for her hands. 'Come here,' he said softly, 'let me hold you.' He tugged at her hands and drew her up into his arms.

Megan leaned her face against his shoulder, a mixture of conflicting feelings raging inside her.

'I love you, Megan. Let's get married.'

Her heart seemed to stop. 'Married?' she whispered, pulling back to look into his face.

He smiled crookedly. 'What we're doing now is no good.' A spark of the old humour glinted in his eyes. 'You won't even stay with me through the night. You get up and go home.'

'You once said you didn't want a placid domestic life. You didn't want the responsibility of marriage, children.'

'I didn't, not then. I was an egotistical son of a bitch. I had the most important thing in life and I wasted it.' He paused. 'When I found out what I'd done, I knew I had to get you back. Somehow.'

'What if you feel trapped after a while? What if you feel I smother you again?'

'I won't,' he said fiercely. 'I promise you I won't.' He lifted her face and kissed her with a tender passion that melted everything inside her. 'Megan, please. Will you marry me?'

She pushed away the warnings and the fears and the doubts. 'Yes,' she whispered.

They couldn't get away with just a quick, simple ceremony. On Bali, there was no such thing as a quick, simple ceremony. Everybody in the village and its surroundings got involved, including the Balinese friends, acquaintances and the people from the flood village. It was not merely a wedding, it was a spectacle, with Balinese dancers in elaborate brocade costumes, *gamelan* music and a Balinese buffet that was a work of art in itself, the food displayed in an artistic range of colours, the dishes decorated with flowers. Megan thanked the gods the Sultan was on home leave in New Zealand, or he would have taken over and made the whole affair into a farce.'

'And this was another reason I wanted to marry you,' Nick told her as they finally made their escape and climbed into the car.

'What?'

He grinned as he inserted the key in the ignition. 'To have a Balinese wedding. With all those longwinded, incomprehensible priestly blessings, we can't fail to be very, very, very happy.'

Megan smiled. 'For a very, very, very long time.'

He squeezed her hand, hard. 'How about for ever?'

Her heart leaped. 'It's a deal.'

They spent a week-long honeymoon in a private, thatch-roofed cottage on an isolated stretch of beach. No *turis* here, no vendors selling songbirds or shells or coconuts. The nearest village was a fifteen-minute walk away.

In the early mornings, they took long, lazy walks along the beach, wading barefoot in the water and picking up shells and small pieces of white coral in a myriad of interesting shapes.

They swam, playing in the waves like children. They made love till exhausted—passionately, playfully, tenderly, whatever fitted the mood. They toured the surrounding countryside and sampled food from local *warungs*, sometimes not sure what it was they were eating, because the local language eluded them. For hours they lay on the beach in the shade of the coconut palms, reading, dozing, talking.

'I don't want to leave,' Megan said drowsily. It was their last day, the last day of a week that had been filled with laughter and joy and passion. A week out of time, a week that had not seemed real, a week like a fairy-tale, and she was the princess and Nick was the prince. She was happy. She was in love. She was the luckiest woman in the world, married to the man she loved.

'We can come back here again,' Nick said, wiping sand off her thigh, then laying his hand on her stomach. 'At least we're not leaving Bali to go back to downtown Buffalo.'

'Thank God,' she muttered. They sky was an endless blue above a placid sea. The sound of the waves made her feel sleepy, but maybe it was the local beer they'd had with their lunch.

Nick's hand was drawing slow circles on her stomach, then moved up to her breast, gently caressing one, then the other. Megan lay still, savouring the feel of his hands on her body. Eyes narrowed against the bright light, she peered at his face. He was very brown, his eyes bluer than ever. She loved this face, this man. She always had, she always would.

'No more lines,' he said, stroking her. 'Brown all over.'

She laughed softly. 'I feel very decadent, lying here naked on the beach.'

He shook his head. 'Not decadent. It's erotic, seductive and utterly enticing.'

Through her lashes she saw his face come closer, then she felt the warmth of his mouth on her breast as he captured her nipple and teased it with his tongue. Suddenly she was no longer sleepy. Small, hot flames began to lick through her blood.

'I want you,' he whispered, sliding up over her and covering her mouth in a wildly passionate kiss.

'Just like that?' she asked with feigned surprise.

He groaned. 'What do you mean, just like that? You've been lying here for the last hour, stark naked in the middle of the day, seducing me with every little move and turn. What do you expect me to do?'

She laughed. 'I hadn't thought about it.'

'Hah! Miss Innocent.' His mouth hovered close to hers, blue eyes laughing. 'You're just lying there in the sand, thinking of nuclear disarmament or what to ask for for Christmas.'

Megan smiled sunnily. 'Right.'

'Liar. I'll teach you.' Nick kissed her deeply, his hands roaming over her body, touching, teasing. She squirmed beneath him, trying to slip away from him, but Nick held her firmly pinned under the weight of his body.

'I'm ravenous,' he whispered.

'For what? Chocolate cake? Dill pickles?'

He lifted his head and looked at her darkly. 'You,' he growled. 'I want to do unspeakable things to that sensational, silky, sexy body of yours.'

'Sandy body, you mean.'

He put a finger across her lips. 'Sshh, don't spoil it. I'm on a winner now.' He nibbled at her ear. 'I'm going to make love to you until you beg, plead and pray for mercy.'

She gave a little shiver of delight. 'Oh, goodie!'

'You are my woman,' he murmured. 'The most beautiful in the world. Your eyes sparkle like champagne. Your hair is like dark silk in the sun.' His hand fondled her breasts with teasing tenderness. 'Your skin is as smooth as satin, as soft as Venetian velvet.'

Megan watched him through her lashes. 'What did you do?

Read the Arabian Nights?'

His mouth silenced her. Then he moved and kissed her eyes, her cheeks, covering them with moist little kisses. 'You taste like strawberries and cream, like double fudge ice-cream, like peach tarts, like May wine. Your mouth is fresh and sweet like a raspberry.'

She moaned in his ear. 'You're making me sick.'

Nick looked up, wounded. 'Am I overdoing it?'

'A bit.' Laughter bubbled up in her throat.

'I thought women liked romantic compliments and flowery talk.'

'With the right touch. I'm afraid you haven't got enough Italian genes in you.'

Nick sighed. 'You may be right.' He took his weight off her and lay on his side, pressing intimately against her. The rough hair of his chest tickling the side of her breast. His hand stroked the length of her leg, her hip. 'My mother traced our family tree. Let's see now.' He frowned in mock concentration, his hand not stopping its sensuous exploration of her body. 'There's some Irish, some Swedish, a touch of German, and way back a loose lady from Liverpool who eloped with a chimney sweep from Milano who pretended to be an Italian count. They had three sons. The first was a gambler, the second a drunkard and the third stowed away on a ship to the New World and made it big in hogs in Iowa. He was one of my great-great-grandfathers on my mother's side.'

'You never told me about that.' Megan slipped a hand over his chest, playing with the whorls of dark hair. Her nerve-endings tingled with his nearness and the anticipation of greater pleasures.

He gave her a solemn look. 'It's a family secret, a dirty little secret. But you're in the family now, so I guess you have the right to know.' His hand fondled her breast, teasing the nipple; the urgency inside her grew, making it harder to talk.

She lifted her arms and ran her fingers gently through

the dark thickness of his hair. 'If I'd known, I'd never have married you.'

Nick have a devilish little grin. 'So it's a good thing I never told you. Imagine what you would have missed! I may not have the words of an Italian, but I do have the touch.'

'Is that right?' Megan looked up into his face. Above his head, the palms moved languidly against the blue sky, a slow, sensuous rhythm of wind and leaves. She moved slowly against him, moving with the swaying palm fronds. 'Show me,' she whispered.

He wasted no more energy on words. There was magic in those big, strong hands, magic and gentleness that made her senses sing. He knew how to touch her—how and where. His kiss was all fire, hot like the sun glittering on the waves as they rolled towards the shore. It brought out in her the most primitive woman, lying naked on the beach in the arms of a man, with the sound of the sea in her ears, wanting nothing but the most primitive pleasures.

Adam and Eve in Paradise. The though flickered through her, and she wondered briefly about serpents and forbidden fruit. It was difficult to think of anything at all as her body was taken over by the mindless pleasure of his touch and the thrills of delight quivering through her limbs.

Nick turned on his back, taking her with him, and she looked down into his smouldering eyes and smiled. It gave her pleasure to touch him in return, to feel the textures of smooth skin, hard muscle and crisp rough hair. His damp skin tasted salty from the sea water as she ran her tongue in little circles over the flat, hard plane of his stomach.

He lay back, eyes closed, giving himself up to her caresses, and she felt a heady sense of power as she watched the strong, virile body tremble under her fingers. His irregular breathing and the frantic beating of his heart under her hands excited her. Flecks of sunlight, escaping through the leafy canopy above, flitted restlessly across his chest—elusive, untouchable.

The sea breeze feathered across her feverish skin, rustling the palm fronds. Nick's sigh, as she kissed him, mingled with the sound of leaves.

'Megan,' he whispered, 'I love you.' His voice was like a sweet caress, the words like rose petals slowly drifting into her heart.

With a ragged breath, he drew her to him and turned her over on her back. He lifted himself up on his arms, hovering over her, breathing hard. His body was rigid, fighting for control. 'Oh, God, Megan,' he said hoarsely. His eyes were dark blue pools, like deep, still water, reflecting her own tremulous desire. She felt the urgent heat of his body as he pressed against her.

'Please, Nick,' she whispered, 'please.' He closed his eyes, and an incoherent sound came from deep in his throat as his body fused with hers. A frenzy took over and, for a moment, breathless, she thought she was drowning. She gasped, opened her eyes wide, and the sun blinded her—white-hot like the fire raging inside her. He groaned and she felt a shudder go through him, finding an echo in the trembling of her body. The sun exploded inside her, a mad swirling of light and fire, and the sound of his voice calling her name.

Then the wildness receded. The shade, cool and soothing, enveloped them, and the waves and the wind whispered a peaceful melody.

'Mrs Nick?'

Megan looked up from her toast, seeing Ibu standing in the door of the dining-room. She wasn't sure where the 'Mrs Nick' had come from, but she didn't mind it.

'*Tukang bunga disini*, the flower man is here. Do you want to buy flowers?'

Every Saturday morning, the flower man passed by the house, his wares in two large ratten baskets hanging from the ends of a long pole balanced across his shoulders.

'No, thank you,' she said, smiling, and returned to spreading jam on her toast.

'Don't you like flowers?' Ibu enquired. 'They're very nice, very fresh.'

'Maybe another time.' Ibu went back into the kitchen, and Nick have her a quizzical look.

'Why don't you buy some? They're cheap enough.'

It was true. For two dollars, she could have flowers in every room of the house. She shrugged. 'I don't feel like getting up right now. I'll get some another time.' The truth was that she hadn't bought flowers once since she'd moved into Nick's house two months ago. She had some sort of mental block and couldn't make herself do it. Neither had she done much to the house itself, but had left it more or less the way it was, furnished with the basics and few frills.

She was too busy to worry much about it. Construction of the houses had begun, and there never seemed to be an end to the work. She enjoyed the job and spent most of her energy on it.

'Have you tried the guava jam?' she asked. 'Ibu just made it yesterday.' She pushed the jar toward him across the table and he took it, frowning at her, but saying no more.

Nick had a meeting with the Govenor on Monday afternoon and came home late. Megan was in the bedroom, putting a new roll of film in her camera, when she heard him come down the hall. He stopped in the bedroom doorway and looked at her, as if waiting for something. He wore dark tailored trousers and a dark, long-sleeved batik shirt, the formal dress of Indonesia.

'Hi,' she said with a smile. 'How was your meeting with the Governor?'

'Interesting, as always.' He did not elaborate.

She advanced the film to the first frame and put the camera down. He was still standing in the doorway, and when she looked up she found him gazing at her with a strange, dark intensity.

She felt a twinge of apprehension. 'Any problems?'

'No.' He closed his eyes briefly and shook his head, as if to brush off some thought or feeling. He advanced into the room, unbuttoning his shirt.

She watched him as he changed into shorts and a T-shirt, wondering what was the matter, and why he had looked at her so strangely as he stood in the doorway.

He went into the bathroom to wash up. When he came back, he moved towards the bed and held out his hands.

'I'm going to find a drink. Coming with me?'

Megan put her hands in his and smiled. 'Sure.'

He drew her up and gathered her against him, lowering his chin in her hair. They stood like that for a long time, then finally he drew away a little, lifted her chin with one finger and kissed her lightly on the lips.

'Let's go,' he said, taking her hand. He looked tired, and she heard a touch of sadness in his voice. Or maybe it was just her imagination.

He brought her flowers a few weeks later, three large pink orchids, delicate and exotic. 'One for every month we've been married,' he said, his mouth tilting in a smile.

She took the flowers from him, feeling touched by his romantic gesture. 'Thank you,' she said huskily. 'They're beautiful. Nobody ever gave me orchids before.'

There was an unfathomable expression in his eyes as he stood there looking at her, and she felt a twinge of unease.

'I'll go put them in water,' she said, heading towards the kitchen.

He took her arm. 'Come here,' he said in a tight, low voice, drawing her into his arms. His mouth was hard on hers, kissing her with a fierce, wild passion that almost frightened her. His arms held her to him with so much strength that it hurt.

'I love you,' he groaned. 'I love you, Megan.' Then he

pulled back and looked at her with fiery eyes. 'Kiss me, Megan,' he said huskily.

She stared at him, clutching the flowers in her hand, then slowly moved one arm around his neck and lifted her face to his, kissing him softly. For a moment he didn't move, his mouth unresponsive, then the hunger was back and he crushed her painfully against him and kissed her fiercely, his mouth hot and searching.

There was an awkward silence after he withdrew. She didn't know what to say. She felt a growing unease at his strange behaviour.

He raked his fingers through his hair. 'I'm sorry,' he said. 'I don't know what got into me.'

Megan wondered what was happening. Over the last few weeks she'd seen the light fading in his eyes. Initially, she'd thought it was her imagination, but now she knew it was not. She didn't know when it had started or what had caused it. She couldn't remember anything inauspicious happening between them. But something had changed and it became clearer every day. Nick didn't laugh as much as he did, he seemed more withdrawn. It had nothing to do with the job; everything was progressing relatively smoothly.

It had something to do with her.

Fear haunted her through the following days. It lay in her stomach like a rock, heavy and immovable. She watched his face, listened to the words he said. She didn't understand what was going on. She knew he wasn't happy, but she didn't know why.

He was as attentive as ever, more than he'd ever been when they'd been together in Washington. He seemed intent on making her happy, pleasing her. He still made love to her with all the ardour and passion he'd displayed on their honeymoon, yet there was less laughter, less playfulness.

Why was there this change in him? Why was there the sadness in his face, those lines around his mouth? Why did he no longer teased her like he used to? Why was he not happy?

At night, it was worst. The questions turned and turned around in her head, until she felt dizzy with fear and wanted to cry out for help.

Something was terribly wrong.

CHAPTER NINE

'YOU'RE not eating.'

Megan stared at the *gado gado* on her plate. The colourful vegetables were artfully arranged, the spicy peanut sauce perfectly seasoned with garlic, soy sauce and hot chilli, yet she had no appetite. She hadn't had an appetite for days. She pushed the bean sprouts around with her fork.

'I'm not hungry.'

'You hardly had a thing at lunch,' Nick said. 'You weren't hungry then, either.' He paused, scrutinising her face. 'Megan, are you all right?'

She shrugged carelessly, ignoring the concern in his voice. 'I'm fine.'

You're not fine, her inner self denied. You're making yourself sick with worry. Do something!

She didn't know what to do. She didn't have the courage to talk or ask the questions, because she was afraid to hear the answers. Why have you been acting so strangely lately? Why don't you make love to me any more?

He hadn't touched her for almost two weeks. Every day, the fear grew sharper. Maybe he didn't love her any more. Maybe he had decided it had all been a mistake. Maybe he was sorry he had married her.

Later that evening, she lay next to him in bed, pretending to read. He was reading too, or pretending as well, she wasn't sure. Despite the night sounds coming in through the open windows, the room seemed oddly quiet. There was no wind and even the sound of water from the brook seemed subdued. Megan glanced over at Nick, his eyes

176

intent on his book. The sheet was pulled up to his waist, his chest bare. She wanted to reach out, touch him, hold him, ask him to please love her, but she felt paralysed with fear.

It was as if, in the stillness of the room, she could feel her thoughts and fears vibrate in the air. Her throat felt thick and painful with unshed tears.

He looked up from his book, as if he'd sensed the strange energy in the room. Their eyes locked and the silence seemed to thicken with tension.

'You're unhappy,' he said.

'You don't want me any more.' Megan's voice shook.

Nick shook his head. 'No, that's not true.'

'We haven't made love for close to two weeks.'

'I wasn't sure you wanted to.'

Megan stared at him. How could he possibly think she didn't want him? Every time they made love, she was eager for his touch, his kisses, his body. 'What made you think that?'

There was quiet despair in his face. 'Because you never tell me you do, Megan. Because you never reach out to me and make me see it in your eyes.' He made a helpless gesture, and the book slid off the bed and fell to the floor with a thump. 'I don't understand you any more. you're not the girl I remember. You used to be a simple person, easy to read.' The memory brought a sad smile to his face. 'It was all in your eyes, in the things you said and did—you never held back.' He paused and there was pain in his eyes. 'Now I see restraint in your eyes and you never touch me any more.'

You never touch me any more. . . Megan said nothing, staring blindly at her hands bunching the sheet between her fingers.

'I remember the times,' he said in an odd, strangled voice, 'when you would take my hand, or just kiss me out of the blue, or touch my arm as you walked by, or smile at me

across the room with that look of love in your eyes. Just
ordinary, casual gestures.'

She remembered, too. She remembered very well. And
she remembered other things—words, painful words. *You
love me too much. You smother me.* In a secret place in her
heart, she had vowed it would not happen again. She would
not love him too much. She would not smother him.

And now he was asking for what he had once rejected.
Anger flared briefly through her—hot, burning. For a
terrifying moment she felt like screaming at him, hitting
him, hurting him. You didn't want me then! You didn't
want me loving you the way I did and now you blame me
for having changed! She choked the words back, and the
desolation in his face made her anger fade.

He averted his face, looking at some invisible spot on the
wall. 'I remember the time you brought me roses,' he went
on. 'A small bunch of tiny red roses. And I felt so guilty,
because I'd never brought you roses and I didn't know what
to say, and somehow you interpreted it as meaning I didn't
like a woman giving me flowers. You got mad and called me
an unliberated male chauvenist, and then you cried and hid
in the bathroom.'

Again a silence, and Megan didn't know how to break it.
An overpowering sadness clogged her throat.

Nick looked tired and drawn. 'When I come home and I
know you're there, I open the door and I wish you'd come
to me and throw your arms around me like you used to do.
But you never do. You smile and you ask me how my day
was and you don't kiss me or touch me. And I always
remember the way it was and I hate myself for doing what I
did to you.'

Megan swallowed the lump in her throat. A thousand
tears seemed lodged there. She knew what it was. It wasn't
because she didn't want to. Every time, she could feel
herself tense with the effort to hold back. No impulsive

hugs, no uninvited kisses, no suggestive candles in the bedroom.

'I'm afraid,' she confessed shakily.

'Afraid of what?' he asked, looking at her with so much despair that her heart ached.

'Of my own feelings.' She closed her eyes, trying to concentrate on her words, the right expression of what she meant. 'I know what I feel for you, and it's what I've always felt for you.' She swallowed again, afraid she couldn't keep the tears back much longer. 'I love you, but . . . but I'm afraid of being vulnerable again. I'm afraid, if I show it too much, you . . . you won't like it. You'll feel like I'm smothering you again.' She bit down hard on her lower lip, forcing tears back. 'I'm afraid you'll leave me again.'

That was why her relationships afterwards with Jason, with David, had been shallow and superficial. It was the reason she couldn't give herself now, not totally and emotionally. It made her feel cheap to want Nick so, yet not to give herself wholeheartedly. Physical love was important, but not the most important. It wasn't good, it wasn't right, but it seemed impossible to deny herself the physical closeness. And at the same time it made her miserable to know she was keeping part of herself from him.

'Megan,' he said with sudden fierceness, 'I won't ever leave you again. I made a terrible mistake three years ago. I should . . .'

She shook her head. 'Maybe it wasn't a mistake, Nick. Your feelings were probably honest enough. I was cramping your style. I was demanding commitments you weren't ready for. The time wasn't right for you.'

'I should have thought it through more! I should have realised what I was throwing away! I didn't know the value of what I had. I want it back, but sometimes I'm so afraid I've destroyed it—something in you. You've changed. You're no longer that warm, loving, spontaneous woman, except . . .' Nick closed his eyes briefly, then looked at her with a terrible hunger in his eyes. 'Except when we make love. When we make love, everything is so good, so . . . perfect between us. Every time, I hope things will change between us in the daytime and I try to make you happy. Nothing seems to work. There is always that little reserve, that distance that I don't seem to be able to cross.' He leaned back against the pillow and threw his arm across his face. His hand was balled into a fist and Megan saw the tenseness in his body.

Then everything began to blur around her, and silent tears slid down her face. 'I'm sorry,' she whispered. 'I'm so sorry I disappoint you.'

'It's not your fault.' He turned to face her. 'Don't cry, Megan, don't cry.' He reached out for her and drew her into the circle of his arms, against the warmth of his body.

But he did not tell her he loved her, and he didn't make love to her.

The next day Megan came home a little early from a trip to the flood village. Nick was not home yet. She went into the kitchen and talked to Ibu, who was busily chopping up red pepper and onions and cabbage leaves.

'I forgot to tell you what we wanted to eat tonight,' Megan said, and Ibu smiled.

'*Tidak apa apa*, it doesn't matter,' she answered. 'I'm making *bakmi goreng*. You like fried noodles, yes?' she asked hopefully.

'I like everything you cook, Ibu, you know that.'

'But not these days. You're not eating.'

'It's not your cooking. I've been very . . . busy.'

Ibu kept her dark eyes firmly on the red pepper. 'You must eat to stay strong.'

'I'm all right, Ibu, don't worry.' Megan fled the kitchen. She took a shower and washed off the day's dust and sweat, then poured herself a glass of sherry and took it to the veranda. She stretched out and tried to relax, but her nerves seemed wound tight as a spring. Normally she enjoyed the late afternoons, when the sun was low and the world took on a golden sheen, but today she saw nothing. There was only the memory of the sleepness night and Nick's pained voice and the hunger in his eyes.

She heard the Mitsubishi drive up to the house, felt her stomach cramp with anxiety. She hadn't seen him all day. Her husband was coming home and she didn't know what to say to him. There were footsteps in the house, but they did not move towards the veranda. A few minutes later, she got up to find him.

He was in the bedroom, sitting on the edge of the bed with his head in his hands.

Fear rushed through her. 'Nick? What's wrong?'

He looked up, and the bleakness in his eyes tore through her. 'I got a telegram just now. My father died—massive heart attack.'

'Oh, no!' she exclaimed.

Nick came to his feet, and she saw the trembling of his hand as he raked his fingers through his hair. 'I've got to go home and take care of things.' He looked around as if in a daze, his eyes unfocused. 'Do you kow where we put the suitcases?'

'They're in the closet in the guest bedroom. I'll get one. When can you get a flight out?'

'Not until tomorrow morning.' He looked at her, his eyes dark in the pale face. 'Can you manage by yourself for a week or so?'

She nodded numbly, and the pain in his face brought tears to her eyes. 'Oh, Nick!' She went up to him and put her arms around him, her head against his chest. 'I'm so sorry. I'm so terribly sorry.'

She felt his body tremble as his arms came around her,

holding her as if she were a lifeline. He took a few steps back, drawing her with him as he sat down at the edge of the bed. He put his face against hers, and they sat like that for a long time. She wondered what was going on in his head. Remorse, regret, guilt? She was afraid to ask.

Finally he looked up. 'I did try, you know, to make peace with my father.' He smiled ruefully. 'You never believed I really tried, did you?'

Megan made a helpless gesture. 'I don't know, Nick. I suppose I shouldn't judge you. I have no way of knowing what went on between you privately. It just always seemed such a shame to me. You know how I feel. I'd do anything to have my father back.'

'But you can't deny your true self for another person, Megan. Not even your own father.'

She put her head on his shoulder. 'But you feel guilty, anyway,' she said softly.

'Yes.'

There were lots of pat answers to this. Guilt is destructive. Guilt like this does not make sense. She said nothing, just held him, and he seemed content to just sit there with her arms around him.

Eventually, a soft knock on the door disturbed the silence, and Ibu's subdued voice announced that dinner was on the table.

Reluctantly, Nick released Megan and came to his feet, holding out his hand to pull her. He drew her back into his arms, holding her so tightly she could barely breathe.

'Thank you,' he said huskily.

The ten days that Nick was gone dragged endlessly. At night, Megan lay awake thinking about him, the bed too empty for comfort.

She knew she loved him.

She knew he wasn't happy with her. His words kept

coming back to her over and over again. 'I'm afraid I've killed something in you. You're no longer that warm, spontaneous woman you used to be.'

For a moment she had forgotten her reserve, had put her arms around him and comforted him. And later, he had said, 'Thank you.' A husband thanking his wife for a simple embrace—it was pathetic. Tears clouded her eyes, and her body tensed with fear. There was always that other time, those other words that got in the way. 'I feel like I'm suffocating. You love me too much. You smother me.'

Had he really changed that much? Did he really want her now, the way she had been then? Like the girl he had rejected?

Well, he had married her, hadn't he? He had developed the largest scheme of all—created a job for her on this exotic island so they could be together again, get to know each other again. Start over. Could there be anything more romantic than that? He'd put his own career on the back burner to be with her, to win her back.

He wanted her back the way she had been. Spontaneous, warm, loving.

Could she find that person again? She was still there, buried behind the memories and the fear, but would she have the courage to let her out? I'll have to, she thought. I can't go on this way, always holding back. I can't go on being afraid. I don't want to be afraid to be myself. And then, unbidden, other words came to her—words he had spoken not in relation to her, but to his father. 'You can't deny your true self for another person, Megan. Not even for your own father.'

It was exactly what she had been doing ever since she'd met Nick again. Out of fear, she had denied her true self, thinking he didn't want her the way she had once been. She had been wrong, terribly wrong, and it had led to nothing but pain for both of them.

She knew that, if she loved Nick and if she wanted to make him happy, there was only one thing to do. She would have to show him her true self.

Megan was early at the airport. The plane was late and the waiting seemed interminable. Then, finally, she saw him, and her heart made a somersault—nerves and love and happiness. He stuck out way above the other passengers, tall and wide-shouldered, his blue eyes searching until the found her. A smile spread across his face.

For a moment, she stood rooted to the ground, fear clutching at her. Then she forced it down with blind courage and ran towards him, throwing her arms around him. No more waiting . . . no more waiting for him to come to her. She pressed herself against him, wanting to feel him, hold him, be close to him.

'I've missed you,' she said against his cheek. And suddenly it was no longer difficult. Suddenly it was the easiest thing to do. She found his mouth and kissed him hungrily, then pulled away and looked into his face. 'I'm so happy your back.' Her voice wobbled and silly tears welled up in her eyes.

Nick looked down at her with the funniest smile she had ever seen. 'I'm happy I'm home, too,' he said huskily, kissing her eyes.

They got his luggage and found the car in the car park.

'Are you tired?' Megan asked.

'Not too bad.'

'I'll drive.' She got in behind the steering wheel. 'You trust me to drive you?'

He gave a crooked smile. 'I trust you with my life.'

'You do?' she asked lightly, smiling.

He nodded, holding her gaze. 'I do.'

He looked wonderful with those lights in his eyes, that funny smile of his. She felt herself swell with her love for him. Yet she noticed, too, the lines of strain and fatigue on his face. He looked older, somehow.

She manoeuvred the car carefully through the busy Denpasar traffic. Another hour and they'd be home. She felt a twinge of trepidation.

'How did everything go?' she asked, after they had left the city.

Nick shrugged. 'As can be expected. There was the funeral and then the meeting with the lawyers and the Board of Directors.' He gave a wry smile. 'The business is mine. I never wanted it, but he gave it to me, anyway.'

'Would it have made you feel better if he'd left it to someone else?'

'Maybe, I don't know.'

'What are you going to do?'

'I left the running of the business in the hands of a managing director. It will be all right.'

There was no one at the house when they came back. No Ibu hurrying out of the door to greet the traveller with a wide smile of welcome.

'Where is Ibu?' asked Nick, looking around, frowning.

'I sent her home. She'll be back tomorrow.'

She didn't want anybody around. Not tonight. Tonight, she was taking care of everything.

They went into the living-room, and she saw the surprise on his face as he scanned the room, taking in the flowers everywhere, the candles ready to be lighted.

'This looks . . . wonderful!' he said.

'Welcome home.' She stood in front of him, put her arms around him and kissed him. 'Now, why don't you have a shower? I'll fix us a drink and then dinner.' She sniffed and grinned. 'You smell like an airplane.

He didn't answer, but crushed her to him and kissed her with such passion that she reeled on her feet. Then he released her abruptly, picked up the suitcase and walked towards the bedroom without a word.

Megan smiled to herself and went into the kitchen to make the last preparations for dinner—his favourite casserole of shrimp and crab. The table was beautiful, with a centre-piece of orchids and tall slender white candles. She'd borrowed some wine-glasses, had even managed to buy a bottle of champagne.

She carried the drinks out to the veranda and Nick joined her not much later. 'Do I smell better now?' he asked, as he bent over her to kiss her.

'Mmm . . . much.'

He sat down with his drink and sighed contentedly. 'There's no place like home,' he commented.

'This is Bali.'

'Home is where the heart is.' He smiled and his eyes shone with warmth and love.

'I'll get dinner on the table,' Megan said after she'd finished her drink. 'Give me five minutes and then come to the dining-room, all right?'

In the kitchen, she took the casserole out of the oven and put it on the table. She arranged the warmed bread rolls in a basket and put that on the table, too. She lit the candles and turned off the overhead light.

Her heart beat erratically as she heard Nick's footsteps coming down the hall. He stopped in the doorway and surveyed the room, taking in the flowers, the wine, the candles.

'This is beautiful,' he said, and there was a strange tone to his voice.

They both sat down, and there was silence for a long moment, as his gaze lingered on the dish in the middle of the table. Then he looked up, and his eyes seemed suddenly very dark.

'I haven't had this since . . . since I left you.' His voice was very low.

'I haven't, either. You remember?'

'Of course. I'll never forget that night.'

Megan swallowed hard. 'Maybe . . . maybe we should start over.'

He nodded, reaching out for her hand while his eyes locked hers. 'Let's do that.'

He released her hand and began to open the bottle of champagne. The cork popped out obediently and he filled the glasses.'

'To us,' he said, lifting his glass. 'To a long and happy married life.'

'Yes,' she said huskily.

Megan had outdone herself on the food. She was no cook but, when she applied herself, miracles came out of her fingers. For Nick, she could do anything. Apparently that, too, had not changed.

Dinner over, she came to her feet, went around the table and stood by his chair.

'Coffee now, or later?'

He moved his chair back and took her hand. 'What would you prefer?'

She sat down on his lap, arms around his neck. 'What I want now is you,' she said in his ear. Her voice quavered, but she forced herself to go on. 'I love you and I want you and I want to make love to you.'

His arms around her back tightened their hold on her, and there was a moment of silence. 'I was afraid I'd never hear to say that again,' he said. 'Oh, God, how I've longed to hear you say that! How I've longed to know whether you made love to me because I wanted to, or because you wanted to.'

'I always wanted to.' She could hear the smile in her own voice.

Nick lifted her chin so he could look at her. 'But sometimes I very much wanted you to come to me, instead of me always doing the inviting.'

'I'm coming to you now.'

'Yes.' And suddenly the grin was back, the lights in his eyes, the joy in his face. 'OK, Meggie,' he whispered seductively, 'let's go to bed.'

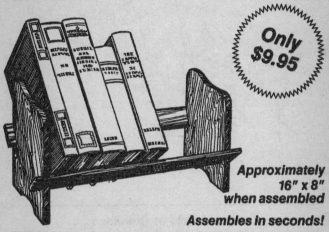